The
Baby
Quest

PAT WARREN

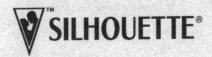

SILHOUETTE®

*All the characters in this book have no existence outside the imagination
of the author, and have no relation whatsoever to anyone bearing the
same name or names. They are not even distantly inspired by any
individual known or unknown to the author, and all the incidents are
pure invention.*

*First published in Great Britain 2001.
Silhouette Books, Eton House, 18-24 Paradise Road,
Richmond, Surrey TW9 1SR*

© Harlequin Books S.A. 2000

*Special thanks and acknowledgement are given to Pat Warren
for her contribution to the Montana Brides series.*

ISBN 0 373 65051 5

19-1201

*Printed and bound in Spain
by Litografia Rosés S.A., Barcelona*

PAT WARREN

had written for two newspapers, and had several magazine articles published before she turned to books. A versatile writer, she's published in contemporary romance, mystery, suspense and mainstream fiction. She's the author of forty-eight novels, and there are over six million copies of her books in print. Pat is a film buff, an avid reader and enjoys taking trips with her travel agent husband. She lives in Arizona and is the mother of four grown children.

MONTANA BRIDES

Twelve rich tales of passion and adventure,
of secrets about to be told...

MONTANA BRIDES
THE KINCAIDS

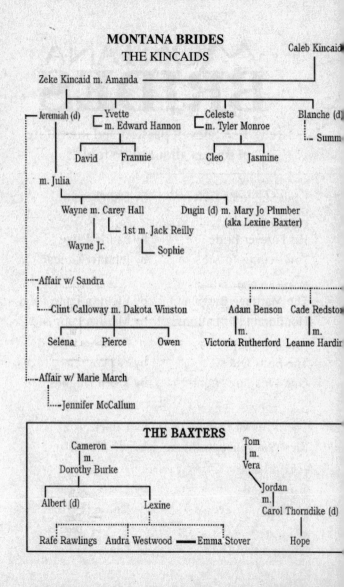

Caleb Kincaid

Zeke Kincaid m. Amanda

Jeremiah (d)   Yvette
     m. Edward Hannon

Celeste
  m. Tyler Monroe

Blanche (d)

Summ

David   Frannie

Cleo   Jasmine

m. Julia

Wayne m. Carey Hall   Dugin (d) m. Mary Jo Plumber
                                                     (aka Lexine Baxter)

           1st m. Jack Reilly

Wayne Jr.

Sophie

Affair w/ Sandra

Clint Calloway m. Dakota Winston   Adam Benson   Cade Redsto

Selena   Pierce   Owen

m.   m.
Victoria Rutherford   Leanne Hardi

Affair w/ Marie March

Jennifer McCallum

THE BAXTERS

Cameron   Tom
   m.   m.
Dorothy Burke   Vera

                                        Jordan
                                    m.
Albert (d)   Lexine   Carol Thorndike (d)

Rafe Rawlings   Audra Westwood ▬▬ Emma Stover   Hope

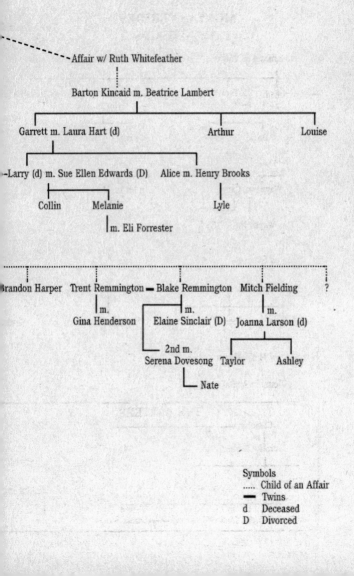

- - - - Affair w/ Ruth Whitefeather

Barton Kincaid m. Beatrice Lambert

Garrett m. Laura Hart (d)   Arthur   Louise

Larry (d) m. Sue Ellen Edwards (D) Alice m. Henry Brooks

Collin   Melanie   Lyle

m. Eli Forrester

Brandon Harper Trent Remmington — Blake Remmington Mitch Fielding ?

Gina Henderson Elaine Sinclair (D) Joanna Larson (d)

2nd m.
Serena Dovesong Taylor Ashley

Nate

Symbols
..... Child of an Affair
— Twins
d Deceased
D Divorced

Prologue

Where was the baby?

That was all Rachel Montgomery could think about.

In the few days since Rachel had learned that her sister Christina's body had been found in a shallow grave, murdered after she'd given birth, Rachel had been obsessed with the baby. Christina's baby. Her niece or nephew…still missing after three months.

It had taken the sheriff's department all that time to locate her sister's body. How long would it take them to find the tiny child? Rachel berated herself endlessly that she hadn't made the time to reach out more to Christina; she wouldn't make the same mistake with Christina's child. That baby had Montgomery blood and it should have their name, too.

Which was why Rachel had taken Deputy Sloan Ravencrest's advice and was on her way to see Winona Cobbs. Folks around Whitehorn believed that Winona, a bit eccentric, was also a psychic. Rachel had always liked her, though she wasn't sure she believed in Winona's powers as many did. But these were desperate times.

Taking a steadying breath, Rachel opened the door to the Hip Hop Café, where Winona was likely to be found. The two large picture windows were steamy and the heat most welcome as she walked in out of the late November cold and looked around. Though she'd been back to Whitehorn only a few times in the past nine years, Rachel had no trouble spotting her target at a back booth, wearing one of her signature long flowing dresses and a shawl.

Winona's blue eyes twinkled in recognition as Rachel stopped at her booth. "Are you back for good this time, Rachel?" she asked in her high-pitched voice.

"No, Winona, just a visit." In fact, this was her second visit in three months. The first had been in September when her father had called to say that Christina was missing. This second was a week's vacation to help her family through the Thanksgiving holiday, which had passed in a cold, quiet, tasteless meal. And that was days before Deputy Ravencrest had called to say Christina had been found, murdered. "Actually," she said to Winona, "I was hoping we could talk."

"Sit, sit." The old woman waved a hand toward the empty seat, several bracelets studded with polished stones and crystals jangling on each wrist. She studied the young woman sitting opposite her with shrewd eyes. "Soon now, I think, you'll be giving it up."

"Giving up what?" Rachel asked, slipping off her leather jacket.

"Living in that godforsaken Chicago. You belong here. Montana's in your blood." Winona adjusted a hairpin that held her long braid fastened neatly around her head.

This wasn't what she wanted to discuss, nor did she wish to contradict the old woman. She changed the subject immediately. "Have you heard that they've found Christina?" She couldn't bring herself to say Christina's body.

"Yes, my dear." Winona reached over to take Rachel's hand in a comforting grip. "I've felt for some time that your sister wouldn't be with us again."

"Winona, they tell me Christina gave birth to a baby around the time she died. I—I hadn't known she was pregnant. I feel so bad that we'd grown so far apart." She blinked back a fresh rush of tears.

"Her pregnancy was no secret. I suppose your father thought it best to shield you. Never a good idea, hiding the truth." The old woman sipped her coffee.

"Do you have any feelings about Christina's death? I mean, can you tell who did this to her? And what about the baby? Where is the baby?" Rachel pushed back her long brown hair with a shaky hand. "I have so many questions."

"I don't have all the answers, child, but I can tell you one thing. That baby is alive and well."

Hope flared in Rachel's eyes. "Really? Are you sure?"

"As sure as I can be."

"Where is the baby?"

Winona shook her head. "I can't see that. But take comfort in knowing the baby's being well taken care of."

"But that baby belongs with us. With me."

Winona rose from the booth. "Maybe in time, child." She slipped out of the booth and left.

Rachel dabbed at her eyes. She so desperately wanted to believe that Christina's child was being cared for, was well and happy...but how much of a psychic's ramblings dare she believe?

"Thought I'd find you here." Ellis Montgomery slipped into the seat Winona had vacated, his blue eyes darting around at the diners as he did so. The portly man in his late fifties was always conscious of his position as mayor of Whitehorn.

"Dad, why didn't you tell me in September that Christina was pregnant?" Her eyes speared him with a look.

He shrugged. "It didn't seem important."

Rachel sat up taller. "Didn't seem important? We've got to find that child. She's our blood. And what of the father? Who is he? We need answers here. Which is why we need a private investigator."

"Now, honey, we've got to be patient and leave these things to the sheriff."

"That's not what you said a few days ago." Disgusted, she wiped at more tears, this time tears of anger. "Don't you want to find the baby? He or she needs us."

He frowned at her. "How do we even know the baby's alive?"

"Winona just said so."

Ellis waved a dismissive hand. "You're listening to some wacko psychic now? Get hold of yourself, Rachel. You're not thinking clearly."

She was thinking clearly, all right. She was thinking she needed to take action on her own. And if her father—and her brother Max—didn't approve, too bad. She'd been making her own decisions for years now, ever since she'd left Whitehorn for college nine years ago.

The mayor glanced toward the door. "I've got to go now. You get some rest." He put on his hat and slid out of the booth.

Rachel didn't bother to stop him. Instead she gazed out the window at a weak winter sun, feeling as bleak and cold as she knew the temperature to be. She could've predicted her father's reaction. Ever the mayor, he lived his life as if he were on a campaign trail, eager to please his constituents and not at all caring about his own family. And her clone of a brother, Max, who'd taken over from their father as president of Whitehorn Savings and Loan, would go along with whatever Dad said.

Fine. She didn't need anyone. She'd hire a private investigator on her own. There certainly weren't any in this one-horse town, but she'd go to the library and look at the listings in Bozeman. Or…

"Pardon me," a softly feminine voice interrupted her thoughts.

Rachel looked up to see a pregnant redheaded woman who'd been sitting at the table alongside her booth. "Yes?"

"I'm Gina Remmington. I saw you at the Hip Hop some months ago, but we were never introduced. I hope I'm not intruding—"

"Not at all. Please sit down." Rachel glanced toward the table and saw the dark-haired man Gina had been with smile at her.

"That's my husband Trent," Gina explained, sitting in the booth somewhat awkwardly due to her advanced pregnancy. "I—I'm sorry. I wasn't purposely eavesdropping on your conversation, but... well, I heard what you said to the mayor." At Rachel's inquisitive look, she went on. "If you're looking for a private investigator—"

Rachel nodded. "I am."

"Well, then, Rachel, I can help you."

One

Rachel Montgomery sat by the fire in the house of her childhood, drying her hair, alone for the fifth night in a row. Her father had had a dinner meeting in town and hadn't wandered home yet, which apparently was a pattern with Ellis. Where, she wondered, did he go every evening, especially on the Sunday night after Thanksgiving?

Actually, she didn't mind. She enjoyed her solitude, even in Chicago in her apartment. Not for days or weeks on end, of course, for she had friends to go out with, to dinner, a movie. She interacted with lots of people in her role as assistant graphics designer at Kaleidoscope, so evenings alone were often welcome. Yet back here in Montana, they seemed more lonely.

Seeking familiar comfort perhaps, she'd taken a long hot bath and wrapped herself in her old chenille robe that she'd found in the back of her closet. Her feet in scruffy Garfield slippers lovingly saved from her teens, she'd come downstairs and made herself a pot of tea before curling up on the couch in front of the fire she'd built earlier. She no longer thought that fires were wasted on one person. In this house, she could shrivel up and blow away waiting for someone to share a fire with.

Since hearing the news that Christina had been found, she'd avoided giving in to the sorrow waiting in the wings to overcome her. While Ellis and Max turned from their memories, Rachel now invited them.

Sighing, she felt regret move through her. So many things to regret. That her father had always been more interested in politics and business than his family. That Max, who'd been a warm, loving brother when they'd been children, had grown into an arrogant workaholic much like their father. That their mother had died four years ago when Christina had been eighteen. Maybe if Mom had lived, Christina wouldn't have become quite so flighty and irresponsible. However, the truth that Rachel had finally had to face was that Christina had been starved for affection and attention since she'd gotten very little from her family, so she'd turned to men and found an unending source.

Why couldn't her family have been more average, more normal? Rachel wondered. The prerequisites had all been in place, the small Montana town where they'd grown up, a place where nearly everyone knew everyone else. Three children born to a fairly well-off family, all attractive and healthy. What had gone wrong? Why had there been so little love, so little communication, growing up in this big rambling house on Sunnyslope Drive? Or was she longing for the impossible dream?

It had probably begun with her parents' marriage. Deidre Montgomery had been a refined woman from a socially prominent Montana family, one who'd enjoyed going to Bozeman to visit old friends, her library circle, her bridge club. What she hadn't enjoyed was her husband.

Rachel sipped her tea, then returned to her hair brushing. She couldn't help but think of Christina. Her sister had been the pretty one with beautiful, thick chestnut hair. She'd been only thirteen when Rachel had left Whitehorn, yet already beginning to develop very feminine curves.

Christina had been difficult, or so Mother had written to Rachel, but she'd been a good kid at heart. But Mother's death had hit her hard and though Rachel had tried during her short visits home, she hadn't been able to reach Christina.

She should've tried harder, Rachel thought now, tightening her lips to hold back a sob. Oh, God, Christina. Why hadn't I reached out more to you? Why hadn't I insisted you come live with me where I could have watched out for you? Would you be alive today, if I had?

The fire slowly dying, Rachel got up to get the poker to spark some embers. The doorbell rang out twice rather insistently. She glanced at the mantel clock. Who'd be dropping by at nine-thirty?

With the damp towel draped around her shoulders, Rachel opened the door just slightly, yet the cold November wind slipped past the tall man standing in the porch light. Her first impression was that he was big, with broad shoulders and long legs. He had on a sheepskin-lined jacket hanging open, seemingly oblivious of the cold night, and neatly pressed jeans. He wasn't from around here, she decided, despite the Western appearance. No one in her hometown wore tassel loafers.

"I'm Jack Henderson," he said, his hazel-green eyes assessing her just as intently as she'd checked him over. "My sister, Gina, said you were in need of a private investigator." His gaze swept over her again from head to foot. "I guess you weren't expecting me."

Rachel wished she could slam the door closed and pretend she hadn't heard the bell. Gina had called yesterday and said her brother was intrigued by the case and would be arriving soon. But Rachel certainly hadn't expected him to show up on her doorstep the very next day. Gina had told her that for the past eight years Jack Henderson had been running a successful P.I. business out in L.A., the same business, in fact, that Gina herself had been a partner in until her pregnancy and marriage to Trent Remmington. Now the only case she worked on was locating the missing seventh illegitimate grandson of Garrett Kincaid, one of Whitehorn's prominent people.

Suddenly conscious of how she must look in her ratty ancient robe, fuzzy slippers, with her damp hair hanging every which way, Rachel felt heat move into her face.

"No, I mean, yes. Gina said you'd be arriving, but I thought you'd call first." With an unsteady hand, she clutched at the opening of the robe at her throat. "It's kind of late."

Jack's lips twitched as he checked his watch. "In L.A., nine o'clock's considered the shank of the evening. I heard you're from Chicago. Isn't it the same there?''

Rachel wanted to remind him that they weren't in L.A. or Chicago, but she knew he wasn't going to go away until she talked with him. ''All right, come on in. For a few minutes,'' she amended, opening the door wider.

Unfortunately, as Rachel backed up, her floppy slippers caught on a throw rug and she felt herself falling. Oh, no! Not in front of this smooth Los Angeles P.I.! But down she went in a heap on the polished floor, landing unceremoniously on her bottom and her bruised dignity. Gazing all the way up the more than six foot length of him, Rachel saw amusement on his tanned face and she felt like bopping him a good one.

''I think I'm going to enjoy working with you, Rachel,'' Jack said, offering her a hand up.

Yesterday on the phone, Jack had listened to Gina outline the Montgomery case. Twenty-two-year-old Christina Montgomery had been missing for three months before her body had been found. Evidence revealed that she'd given birth at the murder scene. The deceased's sister, Rachel, needed help finding the baby. Gina had also mentioned that Rachel, who'd seemed cautious and reserved by nature, was not exactly unfriendly but somewhat distant. As he helped Rachel up from her unexpected fall, Jack wasn't sure ''reserved'' quite described her.

He could tell that she was trying to recapture her dignity by quickly assuming the role of hostess, taking his jacket and leading him into the cozy living room. She needn't have bothered trying to impress him, he found her nervous attempts surprisingly charming.

"Would you like some tea? I just made a pot." She paused in the doorway, ready to dash into the kitchen for another cup.

"Tea." Jack considered the offer, wondering when the last time was that he'd had tea. "Sure. Why not?"

Pausing in the doorway, Rachel watched him sit and make himself comfortable. The couch was big, yet he seemed to take up nearly half. His size was intimidating, even to Rachel's five-six frame. It probably was a plus in his line of work, she thought.

Retreating to the kitchen, she moved to the cupboard and took out another cup before arranging the sugar bowl and a small dish of sliced lemons on her mother's teakwood tray.

Rachel hated to admit it even to herself, but drop-ins made her jittery, especially when the unexpected guest was a ruggedly handsome man with a devilish grin and shoulders a mile wide. She knew this would be the perfect opportunity to interview Jack Henderson as to just how he'd go about finding Christina's baby, and perhaps Christina's killer. If she hired him, they'd be working closely together and she needed to know if they were compatible.

What questions should she ask to discover that? she wondered.

She glanced toward the doorway, then moved closer to the framed mirror on the side wall. Good Lord, her hair resembled a rat's nest and she'd left her brush in the living room. Rummaging through the kitchen drawers, she finally found a broken half of a comb and pulled it through her hair, fixing the mess as best she could. Grimacing at her reflection, she decided that would have to do.

A fleeting memory came to mind of growing up in this house in her teens and her mother's strong warning that neither of her girls was to leave her room unless fully dressed and well groomed, which was how Deidre Montgomery had been raised.

Well, Mom, you should see me now, Rachel thought with a smile.

She picked up the tray, thinking she'd been gone so long that the man must be wondering if she'd run out the back door. An idea, she silently admitted, glancing one last time at her robe, that actually held a lot of appeal about now.

"Here we are," she commented inanely, setting the tray down on the coffee table in front of the couch. Carefully, she poured his tea, refilled her own cup, then turned to poke at the fire.

Jack doubted that Rachel realized that her obviously old and well-washed robe tied so tightly around her slender frame revealed more of her womanly curves than almost anything she could have worn. He crossed his long legs, enjoying the view and wondering when she'd light somewhere. The woman wasn't merely nervous, she was a bundle of nerves. All right, so he should have called, but after he'd checked in to the Whitehorn Motel, he'd decided he'd drive his rental car around a bit, maybe see where the Montgomerys lived. Once out front of the brick two-story with its gabled roof, he'd seen someone in the living room, her back to the picture window, and on impulse had walked up to the front door and rung the bell.

That was when she'd literally fallen at his feet, he thought, hiding another grin as she turned, rejected the couch and sat in a wing chair to the left of the coffee table.

He sent her what he hoped was a reassuring smile. "Gina told me a little about the case, but I'd like to hear your version, if you're up to talking about your sister."

"I guess so. What would you like to know?"

Jack leaned forward, picked up his cup and tasted the tea. Hot and strong, not so bad. A shot of whiskey would have been an improvement on such a cold night. "Well, for starters, what kind of person was Christina? Who were her friends? What were her habits? Things like that. If you decide you want me to work on the case, I'll check with the sheriff's department tomorrow and get specific details of how she died. I'm told they're handling the investigation."

"Yes, they are. Frankly, although they're decent men I've known for years, I don't have much faith in Sheriff Rawlings and his little band of deputies. Christina was missing for three months and they didn't come up with one clue. They found her strictly by accident. There aren't a lot of homicides around here, which is why I don't feel they're very experienced."

Jack sat back and stretched an arm along the top of the couch. "Is it the murderer you want me to find, or your sister's baby?"

Rachel sipped her tea, watching him over the rim of her cup, studying his expression, trying to gauge the type of man he was. She had no interest in working with someone who thought her request frivolous, one who felt she should leave such things to the professionals, as her father did.

"The baby is of primary interest to me. I don't know how much Gina told you, but neither my father nor my brother has much interest in the child, so it'll be strictly me you'd be working for. Do you have a problem with that?"

His brows shot up. "You mean, because you're a woman? No problem here." Jack smiled to reinforce his remarks.

He had a killer smile, his teeth very white in his tanned face, Rachel thought. And she'd bet he knew it.

"How about you?" he asked. "Think you'd have a problem working with me?" His tone seemed to imply that might be the case.

Rachel squared her shoulders. "None whatsoever." In her career, she'd worked with all sorts of men and women; she certainly could handle a private investigator, even if he was tall, good-looking and a little off-putting.

She set her cup on the coffee table and got down to business. Since he was here, they might as well get started. In short order, she gave Jack a little background about Christina as a sweet child, then becoming somewhat wild as a teenager, having lots of boyfriends, being irresponsible. "She liked to have fun, you know. But all that aside, she was a nice girl with a good heart who was looking for love and friendship and got in with a rough crowd.''

Jack nodded thoughtfully. It had been his experience that relatives couldn't always give the best analysis of a troubled person, especially a sister who'd been gone for nine years. "Living in Chicago as you have been, you probably don't know many of her friends, then, right?"

"No, but I'll find out and make up a list. Whitehorn's a small town, one where nearly everyone knows everyone else. While it's true I've been gone, most of the same people live here as when I left, with a few new arrivals, of course.'' She picked up her cup and drank more tea, glancing at him again. "Do you need to take notes or anything?'' She wasn't sure how P.I.s worked, but surely he didn't rely on his memory?

"Not just yet. Do you know offhand if your sister had any enemies?''

Rachel winced at the thought. Obviously someone had struck that fatal blow to Christina's head, or so the sheriff's department insisted. It was just hard for her to imagine anyone disliking Christina enough to want her dead. "Actually, I don't. She was an even-tempered person, not really argumentative.''

"A party girl? One who drank, maybe too much occasionally?''

Rachel pressed her lips together, annoyed at the question and annoyed because she didn't know the answer. "I suppose that's possible,'' she admitted, fighting the well of tears building at the back of her eyes. "As I said, she liked to have fun, but that's no reason for someone to kill her.'' She swallowed around the lump in her throat and quickly lowered her gaze to the cup in her hand.

She had beautiful eyes, he thought, an interesting blue, very expressive. Right now, tears swam in them, ready to fall. Jack decided to change course. ''Would you happen to know who fathered her baby?''

Sadly, Rachel shook her head. ''No, I don't. If she was seeing someone regularly, I don't know that, either. I've talked to a few people, including a woman who's known around here as something of a psychic.'' She looked up, but his expression hadn't changed. ''I imagine you find that a bit odd, and so do I, actually. But Winona Cobbs' predictions have often come true. And her niece, Crystal, was the one who had a vision as to where the body might be located.''

What had he gotten into here? Jack asked himself silently. He regarded the woman in front of him. Despite the grandmotherly attire, she was softly pretty with intelligent eyes and an oval face that seemed to reveal her every emotion. And she had plenty of them skittering across her features tonight.

Yet he could see that Gina, though she'd just met Rachel, had pegged her pretty well. Rachel was hesitant, reticent, as well as vulnerable, which wasn't surprising given the circumstances. She was struggling with grief over her sister's senseless death and anger at the perpetrator as well as concern for Christina's child. He also thought he sensed a bit of guilt over her not being available to watch out for her sister.

''Do you believe in visions?'' he asked softly.

Rachel sighed, feeling indecisive. "I'm not sure. It's hard to argue with success though, even if it's only occasional."

"That's true." He paused, gathering his thoughts. "So, Christina'd been missing since late August, no one apparently knew if she was involved with anyone, yet she died shortly after giving birth to a child. She didn't live here with your father and though he knew she was expecting, he didn't know who she was seeing. Your brother Max lives not far away and wasn't close to Christina, either."

Rachel crossed her arms over her chest. "You make it sound as if no one in the family cared about her, and that isn't so. After Mom died, Christina changed, became moody, headstrong, difficult. She moved out, began running with a wild crowd. I tried talking with her by phone and on my visits. I even invited her to live with me in Chicago. She told me she was having too much fun just now to leave."

Jack didn't comment, just filed all that away. He'd pushed her a little and gotten her to open up, to reveal more of the truth. Up to then, it had sounded as if Christina Montgomery had been some sort of flawless saint that someone had accidentally, senselessly killed. She may have been well liked, but someone hadn't cared for her, he thought. Someone had killed her.

But he'd heard enough for one night, and he didn't want to upset Rachel further. "I'd like to work on the case, if you want my services."

Jack was a little rough around the edges. But then, Gina had said he'd been a cop in L.A. for years. Ra-

chel would have much preferred an older man with a
lived-in face and a paunch, one far less attractive. Not
that she was ready to fall at his feet—again—but
working with a middle-aged man was less distracting.
However, she didn't have a lot of choices.

"Yes, I'd like that."

"All right, then. I'll start tomorrow. I'll want to
talk with your father and brother, and hopefully you'll
have that list of her friends for me by then." He rose,
ready to leave, to go back to the motel to think things
through.

Rachel remained seated. "Perhaps I didn't make
myself clear, I intend to work *with* you. I plan to call
Chicago and arrange a leave of absence. This baby is
very important to me. I also know this town and
nearly everyone in it. The investigation will go more
quickly if we work together."

Jack turned to face her. "Perhaps *you* didn't understand. I work alone. Even when Gina was at the
agency, we had our separate cases."

She nodded indulgently. "That's fine, but I *need* to
do this with you." She raised her eyes to his, im-
ploring, beseeching. "I made mistakes with Christina,
as you've probably guessed. I don't want to mess up
with her child. I will concede to you being in charge.
But I won't sit here and wait for results. I want to be
with you on this every step of the way."

Jack saw the determination in her eyes and something more. The vulnerability he'd spotted before. He
would have turned down a stubborn, insistent woman
needing to have her own way. But he, too, had made
mistakes in relationships and knew he'd give a lot to

be able to make up for them in some small way. He couldn't deny Rachel a chance to make amends to her dead sister.

"All right, but let's remember, we do it my way. I'm the one with the experience here. All right?"

She found her second smile of the evening. "All right." She got up and walked to the door with him. She was reaching for his jacket on the wooden coat tree when a key turned in the lock and the door swung open.

Ellis Montgomery stepped into the vestibule, his quick glance taking in the tall, broad-shouldered stranger and his daughter wearing a nearly threadbare old robe and disreputable slippers.

"Well, good evening. Rachel, you didn't tell me you'd be entertaining tonight." His voice was cool and combative.

Rachel felt heat move into her face at her father's quick critical judgment, as usual, without knowing the facts. "Dad, this is Jack Henderson, Gina's brother. Gina's married to Trent Remmington, you may recall." She purposely mentioned Gina's husband, who was a wealthy oil investor, knowing such things impressed Ellis. "Jack's a private investigator from Los Angeles. I've hired him to try to find Christina's baby and the person who killed her."

Taken aback, Ellis still didn't offer his hand, instead busied himself hanging up his coat. Ignoring the newcomer, he turned to his daughter.

"I told you to let sleeping dogs lie. The sheriff and his deputies are well qualified and will get to the bottom of all this. We don't need outsiders here med-

dling in our personal affairs." Ellis stroked his black
hair, which his hat had smashed down, and glanced
at Henderson. "Sorry to have you come all this way
on a wild-goose chase. My daughter's upset, as we
all are. But we'll take care of our own problems."

Embarrassed at her father's bad manners as well as
his pigheadedness, Rachel touched his arm as he
started to walk past her. "I'm sorry you feel that way,
Dad, but I've hired Mr. Henderson and I intend to
work with him until this matter is resolved."

Watching the interplay between father and daughter, Jack had to admire Rachel's spirit. She might be
reserved, but she knew what she wanted and she
wasn't about to back down, even as her father glared
at her.

Ellis made a disapproving sound. "Do as you
please, but you're wasting your money." Moving to
the stairway, he spoke to Jack over his shoulder.
"You'd better be going back home. We have a tight-
knit community here and they don't open up to
strangers." He paused, his eyes examining his daughter from head to toe. "Rachel, maybe in Chicago
women entertain men in their nightclothes, but I
thought we'd taught you better." With that, he
marched upstairs and left them staring after him.

Furious at that last remark, Rachel nevertheless
kept her cool. "Jack, I apologize for my father. He's
very set in his ways. I was afraid he'd react like this,
but I should have warned you."

She had lovely skin, Jack noticed, even flushed in
anger. He wished he knew her well enough to at least
take her hands and reassure her, but instead he

shrugged into his jacket. "Don't worry on my account. I've dealt with worse." He stopped, studying her a moment. "Are you sure, in light of your father's strong feelings, that you want to go ahead with this?"

"Absolutely." She glanced up the stairs just as a door slammed. "I don't know if Gina mentioned that Dad's the mayor of Whitehorn. He's every inch a politician, one who doesn't want to ruffle any voter's feathers. Questioning people around town, stirring things up, worries him. Heaven forbid he should lose a vote. But don't worry, please. I can give you a rundown on the part my father played in Christina's life without his cooperation. And, I should further warn you, my brother will react pretty much the same. Max is Dad's clone."

"He's president of the Whitehorn Savings and Loan, right?"

"Yes, the bank Dad started."

"Maybe we should start by questioning him tomorrow. I like to interview family members first, not because they're suspects necessarily but because they can give me insight into the victim's life."

Rachel sighed again, thinking there was apt to be a lot of dirty linen aired before all this was over. Well, so be it. She had to know what happened to Christina and, even more important, she had to find her sister's child.

She held out her hand. "Thanks for coming so quickly."

He took her small hand in his much larger grip, acknowledging silently the softness of her skin, just as he'd suspected. "You're welcome." He held on a shade too long, then let go and opened the door.

Surprised at how the touch of his fingers on hers had her pulse speeding up, she stuck both hands into her pockets. "What time do you want to get started?"

"How would it be if I pick you up at eight? I'd like to have breakfast at this place called the Hip Hop Café. Gina tells me half the town stops in there almost daily. You could fill me in on anyone there who might be important to our case."

"That's fine. I'll be ready."

Despite the chilly air whirling in, Rachel kept the door open a crack as she watched him pull away in his rented Lincoln. First-class all the way, and on her expense account. She wondered if he was staying with Gina and Trent Remmington since they certainly had plenty of room, from what she'd heard. Or had he checked into the Whitehorn Motel? It was decidedly not first-class, but the only place around for miles. If she had to guess, she'd say the latter, for despite the lack of amenities, Jack Henderson struck her as the independent type who needed his own space.

Rachel cleaned up the tea things, checked the fire and set the coffeemaker to start at seven the next morning. Even though they were going to breakfast first, she'd need a little caffeine to jump-start the day. Besides, she told herself, Dad might want some. Though as angry as he was, he might just head out early.

Climbing the stairs, she went over the evening, feeling odd that Jack had learned a great deal about her and her family in a short time, and she knew absolutely nothing about him except his occupation and that he was Gina's brother. Before this was over, she'd probably learn more, though why that should matter, she couldn't say. Simple curiosity, most likely. And because Jack Henderson was different than anyone she'd ever met.

Nevertheless, theirs was only a business arrangement.

Rachel wandered over to the window and stood gazing out, something she was prone to in Montana and seldom ever did in Chicago. It was a cold, crisp night but it wasn't snowing, even though the dark sky was heavy with clouds. Life was so different here, much slower-paced, more laid-back. She'd hated that as a young woman, impatient to get going, to experience life. But now, though she'd probably not admit it out loud, there was much appeal to a quiet way of life. Fight it though she may, nowhere else had ever seemed like home but this vast big-sky country.

Closing the drapes and getting under the covers, Rachel told herself that she just viewed her hometown differently after nearly ten years away. Not that she'd ever come back.

The Whitehorn Motel was like so many other inexpensive chain motels, Jack thought, entering his room. It was clean, spacious and comfortable. Luxurious it was not, with its TV bolted to a shelf attached to the wall, its skimpy towels and one small cube of soap. However, he'd stayed in worse.

He tossed his jacket onto the lone chair, his keys

onto the bedside table. Gina had invited him to stay with her and Trent if he took the case, but he preferred an anonymous room. Sometimes things got hairy when he searched out killers, and he didn't want to bring any trouble to their home. Also, he'd likely be coming and going at all hours, which would disturb them.

But he'd miss Gina's homecooking, he thought. He'd had lunch in L.A. before leaving and thought he'd grab a bite somewhere in Whitehorn for dinner. But by the time he'd left Rachel's, there was nothing open. He'd have to keep in mind that Whitehorn didn't have the plethora of open-all-night eateries like L.A.

Stifling a yawn, he sat on the bed and picked up the phone to call Gina as he'd promised. She answered on the first ring, as if she'd been waiting for his call. "I hope I didn't keep you up," he said, checking his watch and noticing it was well past eleven.

"No, I'm watching Jay Leno. Can't get to sleep because the baby's really moving around tonight. How'd things go with Rachel?"

"Good." He told her about their visit, leaving out the fall since he was sure Rachel wouldn't want that to get around, and ended with the mayor's arrival and his less-than-enthusiastic welcome.

Gina put the television on mute, noticing that her husband alongside her in their king-size bed was already sound asleep. "I'd heard that Ellis Montgomery wasn't for change or disturbances, that he liked the status quo. I don't know Rachel well at all, but she didn't strike me as the type who'd knuckle under. Did she?''

Jack stretched out on the bed, cradling the phone in the crook of his neck. "Not at all. She's spunky, stood right up to him, but in a respectful way even though he was downright insulting." Especially, he reminded himself, the unnecessary remark about her entertaining in her robe.

"I feel bad for Rachel having to dredge up all the gossip about Christina," Gina said.

"Was she as wild as Rachel said?"

"I haven't been here all that long, as you know, but everyone says she had a whole string of boyfriends. She was a beauty, so it's small wonder."

"There're lots of beautiful women in the world and they don't all become wild. What do you think did it for Christina?"

"Several things I've heard. Her sister, the one ally in the house leaving, then her mother dying. Her father and brother not warm, fuzzy people. Suddenly she blossomed physically and men noticed. Probably went to her head. A sad story."

"Yeah, it is. Rachel's not like that at all. She's attractive, but she seems very grounded. Almost too responsible. I think she feels guilty for not being there for her sister and now wants the baby so she can make amends."

"I agree. I hope you can point out that Christina's spiral down was no one person's fault." Gina paused, and Jack could hear her readjusting her pillows. "Did you two hit it off?"

Did he detect a hint of matchmaking in his sister's

tone? Gina had been trying to get him to quit the L.A. rat race and join her in heavenly Montana—her words, not his—ever since her marriage. "Oh, yeah. She fell for me like a ton of bricks." He smiled at the private joke.

"Oh, you! Be nice to her, Jack. I think she's hurting. And no funny business, eh?"

"Funny business?" He feigned indignation. "You wound me, Gina. You think I'd rush into town and coax a vulnerable woman into my bed just for sport?"

"Yes, I think that's a fair assessment. Reel in your libido. I live in this town."

Though he was eight years older than his sister, now that Gina was married, she seemed intent on keeping him on the straight and narrow, something that amused Jack no end. "I'll keep that in mind. I'd better hit the hay now. I'm picking her up at eight for breakfast at the Hip Hop."

"So you are taking the case?"

"Just until I can get Rachel Montgomery into the sack," he said, knowing his statement would get a rise out of her.

"Stop that! I mean it."

"Just kidding. I'll behave. I'll drop in soon. Say hi to Trent for me. Good night."

Jack hung up the phone thoughtfully. He had been kidding for, as attractive as Rachel undoubtedly was beneath that silly robe, he had an ironclad rule about not mixing business and pleasure. One he had yet to break.

Of course, there was always a first time.

Two

Despite the early hour, the Hip Hop was hopping. Coffeepots were passed around, emptied and refilled often; bacon, eggs and pancakes hissed on the griddle, and Willie Nelson twanged from the jukebox about going on the road again. Rachel led Jack to a back booth where they could observe without being in the front line.

Of course, as the new man in town, Jack was given the once-over from every table, heads turning, folks conjecturing. When someone remembered seeing him at Gina's wedding, they next speculated as to why he was back in Whitehorn and what he was doing with Rachel Montgomery.

"Small towns," Jack commented, picking up the plastic-covered menu as he watched first this person then that send him a curious look. "They're all alike. Knowing everyone else's business is more than a hobby or pastime. It's an obsession."

"Yes, it's one of the reasons I moved away," Rachel answered, studying her menu, realizing it had scarcely changed over the years. "Buckwheat pancakes. Can't find those on just any menu."

Jack decided the view across from him was far more interesting than the menu. Rachel Montgomery cleaned up well, he thought, his lips twitching. More than well. The sun drifting in through the picture windows brought out the red highlights in her shoulder-length brown hair, making it look a lot different than last night.

Her outfit was a far cry from her ratty robe, too. She had on a gray wool sweater with black pleated and cuffed slacks that he was certain no store in Whitehorn was selling. The only jewelry she wore was a ring on her right hand, a black pearl set in chunky gold. But it was her eyes that captivated him—dark blue, almost midnight-blue, eyes a man could drown in.

It occurred to Jack that the heads that had turned were probably looking at Rachel rather than at him.

"Menus can tell you a lot about a place and a location," he commented, dragging his attention away from her. "Mahimahi in Hawaii. Dim sum in Hong Kong. Lamb in New Zealand."

Rachel raised her eyes to his face and noticed for the first time the small scar on his chin. It gave him a rakish look, a dangerous bent. "You've been to all those places?"

"And many more, courtesy of Uncle Sam. I was in the navy for four years. They're right. You get to see the world, although not exactly first-class."

A waitress came over, interrupting their conversation to bring water and setups and to take their order. Because she lingered, Rachel introduced Janie Carson Austin to Jack. As the waitress/manager walked away, Rachel smiled. "She probably wanted to verify your name since she's being asked who the new man in town is.''

"And here I thought they were all buzzing about you," he told her. "You look terrific this morning."

"In contrast to last night, you mean? Anything would be an improvement, I'm sure."

"Oh, I don't know. That robe kind of grows on you. And the slippers—they're collectibles, I'll bet."

She cocked her head at his teasing tone. "Are you making fun of me?"

He held up a hand, palm-out, and shook his head. "Heaven forbid. But your outfit sure set your dad off."

She felt the need to explain a little about her family. "We had a rule when I was growing up, you see. No one left his room unless fully clothed. My mother was a stickler for protocol. She came from this socially prominent family and manners were of the utmost importance to her. As for Dad, he never paid much attention to any rule, until last night, scolding me as if I were seventeen instead of twenty-seven. Apparently, you're always a child to your parents."

"Did he ask you any questions this morning?" Or maybe apologize?

"He was gone by the time I went downstairs. Is your father overly protective or overly nosy, or does that happen only in my family?" All right, so she was curious about him. She felt the need to get to know him a bit if they were going to be working closely together, especially since he'd soon know a great deal about her family.

Jack shrugged. "I don't know much about fathers

since mine deserted us when I was twelve and Gina only four. My mother remarried when I was eighteen, moved to L.A. and took Gina with her, at which time I rushed off and joined the navy.'' He'd left out a lot, but then, he'd never been one to talk much about himself, especially to someone he'd just met.

''Do you see your mother often?'' She was curious whether or not he was a loving son or an indifferent one, although it was none of her business really.

''Not often. She's made a new life for herself and seems happy enough.''

A private man who didn't want to reveal too much, Rachel decided. Maybe he had some skeletons in his closets. We all have a few, she thought.

Their breakfasts arrived—bacon, eggs and toast for Jack and an English muffin and coffee for Rachel. Spreading jam on his toast, he glanced at her skimpy fare. ''Do you always eat like a bird?''

''No. I usually have fruit with my muffin, but there wasn't any on the menu.''

''Oh, well, that's different.'' He took a hearty taste, then glanced around the room casually, thinking everyone should be through discussing them by now. ''So, is there anyone here you'd like to tell me about, someone who might know something about our case?''

The door opened just then and an attractive couple walked in from the cold, the woman a willowy, dark-haired beauty and the man in a sheriff's deputy uniform. Rachel caught the man's eye and waved. ''That's Sloan Ravencrest and Crystal Cobb.''

Jack reached for a piece of bacon and glanced over

his shoulder. "The deputy and one of the women who have visions, right?"

"Yes, and her aunt, Winona, is in the far booth, where they're headed."

For a moment or two Jack studied the older woman wearing some sort of long filmy dress before commenting. "She live around here?"

"Outside of town in a trailer. She has a junkyard business called Stop-n-Swap. Does fairly well, from what I hear. She's the psychic I spoke to about Christina's baby."

Jack took a swallow of coffee. "And you believe her?"

"I want to. I want to believe that child's alive and being well taken care of until I can find him or her."

"And then what?" he asked.

It was Rachel's turn to shrug. "I'm not sure. I only know I want that baby. She belongs with us."

There was no "us," Jack wanted to remind her. Ellis Montgomery didn't seem the sort who'd welcome his dead daughter's illegitimate child. Not politically correct. He'd yet to meet Max, but Rachel had said her brother usually agreed with their father. So it would be all her.

"Would you give up your job in Chicago, move back here and raise the child? Or would you take the baby there and fit it into your life? And what if the father shows up?"

Wiping her mouth on the paper napkin, Rachel leaned back. "I guess I'll face those issues when I must. For now, your job is to find that baby."

"Okay." He finished his coffee and signaled for

the check. "No one else in here I should know about?"

Rising, Rachel shook her head. Walking to the door, she heard her name called and turned to see an old high school friend, Connie Emerson, just finishing her breakfast. Rachel leaned down for a quick hug. "How are you, Connie?" she asked.

"Doing okay." Still single, like Rachel, Connie had left Whitehorn and gone to Billings for a couple of years, but she'd come back. "I heard about Christina. I'm so sorry, Rachel."

"Thanks. It was quite a shock." She'd seen Connie when she'd been in Whitehorn in September, but only briefly. "Did you know she was pregnant?"

Connie's dark brown eyes were serious. "Yes. I haven't heard—did they find the child?"

Rachel shook her head, then nodded toward Jack who was at the cash register paying the bill. "I've hired a private investigator to find the baby."

"Oh?" Connie glanced at the tall man, then raised a brow. "Nice. How long are you staying this time? Can we get together for dinner or a drink?" Connie, who worked at the Whitehorn Insurance Agency, lived in a condo on the outskirts of town.

Rachel noticed that Jack was finished and waiting for her. "I'll be here awhile. I'll call you." They'd kept in touch by mail and the occasional call, but Rachel couldn't help thinking it would be fun to have a long visit with an old friend. Girl talk might take her mind off the reason she was in Whitehorn.

Following Jack outside, Rachel buttoned her

leather jacket against the cold and saw Jack do the same.

"Where to?" he asked, wondering if last night's schedule had changed.

"Let's go visit my brother at his bank," she answered, sliding into his sleek gray Lincoln. Her stomach in knots at the thought, Rachel was glad she hadn't had a large breakfast. She was certain that Ellis had already contacted Max and probably exaggerated last evening's events. She was not in the mood for more criticism just now.

Maybe Max would surprise her and be welcoming.

Max Montgomery kept them waiting for exactly half an hour.

By the time his fiftyish secretary said that Mr. Montgomery would see them now and ushered them down the carpeted hallway, Rachel was fuming inside but apologetic on the outside.

"He's very busy, I'm sure," she whispered to Jack. "I knew we should have called first, but I didn't."

He leaned down to her. "Do you always take the blame on your own shoulders for things that are out of your control?"

Frowning up at him, she wondered if that was how he saw her. And then wondered if she did have a habit of doing that.

Walking in through the door Mrs. Redden, the secretary, held open, Rachel greeted her brother as she strolled over to his large cherrywood desk. The office wasn't huge, but well appointed, the focal point being the back wall of floor-to-ceiling windows with a great

view of the mountains in the distance. Max had re-
modeled the room since her father had used it, choosing plush gray carpeting and muted blue chairs.

"Good morning, Rachel," Max said, then turned
his gaze to her companion.

They were fairly matched in height and weight,
Jack thought, approaching. Rachel's brother had black
hair worn short, a square, handsome face and steely
blue eyes that displayed all the warmth of a Montana
winter. He was wearing a well-cut black suit with a
white shirt and striped tie. Make that a bolo tie and
add a vest and he'd be his father's clone, Jack thought
as he held out his hand.

"I'm Jack Henderson. Thanks for seeing us on
such short notice," Jack said, relieved when Max
reached over to shake hands. Since he hadn't exactly
hit it off with Ellis, he'd like not to start off on the
wrong foot with his son. "It's good of you to take
time from your busy day." However, he couldn't help
noticing that the only things on Max's desk were a
gold pen set, a blotter and a phone. No framed pictures, no papers or file folders.

"I've met your sister," Max said. "She's very
nice." To say nothing of her husband's several accounts at the Whitehorn Savings and Loan, Jack muttered to himself.

"Please, sit down," Max said, sitting back in his
leather chair, his cool gaze moving to Rachel. "I
thought Dad told you we didn't need a private investigator, that we should leave the matter to the professionals."

So he'd already talked with Dad and knew who

Jack was, Rachel noted. "The police and the sheriff's department in this town couldn't locate Christina in three months. Jack's a professional, too, with eight years' experience on the L.A.P.D. and five with his own firm."

Jack decided he'd let them duke it out while he studied Max.

"It would seem you've made up your mind, then." Leaning back, Max braced his elbows on the armrests and steepled his fingers as he eyed Jack. "What do you need from me?"

Jack crossed his legs, feigning casual relaxation in the face of Max's posture of self-importance. "Anything you think might help us to learn more about Christina's habits…who her friends were, places she frequented, that sort of thing."

"I'm twelve years older than Christina, Mr. Henderson. We hardly had the same circle of friends. She was popular, that I'm sure you've heard. After our mother died, she moved out of Dad's house and didn't want much to do with either of us. That's about it."

"Did you try, Max?" Rachel asked quietly. "Did you try to get close to her?"

The flush of anger colored his handsome features, and something else. Resentment or perhaps guilt. "Did *you?*" he parried.

"Not enough, I regret to say."

"Exactly." Max shot his cuffs and checked his slim gold watch. "I'm afraid I've got a meeting in thirty seconds. I'm sorry."

Jack thanked him and shook hands again while Ra-

chel walked out without another word. They were
seated in Jack's Lincoln before either of them spoke.

"That went well, don't you think?" Jack asked,
hoping to lighten her mood.

Staring out the car window unseeingly, Rachel
shook her head. "I don't know whatever happened to
the big brother I used to adore."

"Hard to tell what goes wrong in families," Jack
said, turning on the engine so the heater would kick
in. A Californian, he wasn't crazy about the cold
weather. "Sometimes people just grow up and
change, or we don't notice their true personalities until we're older." For a moment he wondered if Gina
had ever felt that he'd changed, perhaps after he'd
been discharged from the navy. He surely had when
he'd quit the police force, having seen far too much
brutality, man's inhumanity to man. Yet the changes
in him hadn't seemed to affect his relationship with
Gina.

"No, something happened when Max was away at
college. Up to then, he was a happy guy, laughing,
rarely serious. I know he got involved with a woman
up there." Rachel knew firsthand how tragic college
romances could be. Take her and Richard's— No, she
would *not* go there. She'd keep focused on Max. "I
don't know what happened between them. When he
came home, he was a changed man and not for the
better."

"Don't worry about it. Since he rarely saw Christina, there's little he could tell us anyhow."

"I suppose you're right." She sighed, vowing not
to let Max spoil the rest of the day.

"Where to next, boss?" he asked jokingly.

She raised a brow as she turned to him. "I thought you told me you had to be in charge?"

"I'm the director, but you're the boss. Man or woman, the person who pays the freight is the boss."

He had her smiling at that. She had to admit he looked very L.A. today, with his olive-green silk cashmere sweater that brought out the green of his eyes, his designer jeans and hiking boots. And he wore a leather jacket much like hers. Plus, there was that dynamite smile.

Resolutely, Rachel dragged her attention back to the matter at hand. "I think we need to visit the scene where they found her," she said, her voice soft.

Exactly what he'd have said. "Right you are, boss," Jack told her, shifting into gear.

"And don't call me boss."

The wind had picked up by the time they arrived at the mountainous area that Sloan had told Rachel was the place where Christina had been found. Jack pulled the big Lincoln off onto the shoulder of the road and helped Rachel out. They started up the winding dirt path.

"Everything around here looks the same," he commented, squinting as he gazed around. "How do you know we're going the right way?"

"Because I lived in this area for eighteen years. Winter and summer, I've climbed these hills." Glad she'd worn her boots, Rachel watched where she was stepping. Remnants of an earlier light snowfall could be seen in patches here and there between the scraggly bushes and the barren trees. Montana had yet to have its first big snowstorm of the winter.

Walking easily behind her, Jack let her study the terrain while his eyes stayed fastened to her slender frame. She moved gracefully, as if she climbed mountains every day, not a bit winded though the incline became steeper the higher they went. "You must work out at a gym back in Chicago, eh?" he asked, curious about her life back there.

"No, but I walk everywhere. I don't own a car." She ducked under a low-hanging branch, following the path around a bend. Glancing over her shoulder, she saw that he was keeping up without strain. "How about you? Do you get much exercise?" He certainly looked to be in excellent shape.

"I like to drive to the ocean, park and run along the sand. I try to do that two or three times a week."

"Mmm, I'd love to live near the sea."

"Why don't you move?"

Why hadn't she moved? She certainly wasn't tied to Chicago. "Maybe I will one day." Rachel spotted a hawk circling the sky and stopped to admire the fierce bird. "He's something, isn't he?"

Moving up behind her, Jack followed her gaze. "Yeah, creatures of prey usually are fascinating. But very dangerous."

Turning, she realized he was closer than she'd thought, close enough for her to smell the clean masculine scent of him. "Not just in the animal kingdom. That goes for people, too."

His eyes met hers and there was laughter in them. "You think dangerous men are fascinating?"

"I don't know any really dangerous men." But there were all sorts of danger, such as a fatal attraction to the wrong man. Hadn't she been there and done that once already?

"Maybe you do, but you don't know he's dangerous because he's smart enough to hide that element of his nature." Her hair was blowing in the wind, several strands whipping across one silken cheek. He wanted badly to reach up and fix that, to stroke her face. But he sensed she'd back away if he did.

"Are you referring to yourself as dangerous?"

Taking a step back, Jack smiled. "Who, me? Lady, I'm a pussycat."

"Uh-huh. And I'm the Queen of England." She resumed walking.

Several minutes later, the path led into a shallow canyon. Just ahead they could see the yellow crime scene tape stretched across an opening. Slowing her steps, Rachel approached the narrow crevice. Suddenly, her hands were damp and yet she felt a chill.

Jack came up behind her, sensing her emotions were getting the best of her. Gently, he touched her shoulder. "Why don't you wait here and let me take a look?"

"No, I want to see." Her steps sluggish, she moved forward, then stopped and gazed down. The shallow grave was barely a foot wide and perhaps five feet in length. Christina had been small, about five-four, yet even so, it would have been a tight fit. A surge of emotion swamped her, imagining her beautiful sister crammed into that cold, harsh place, lying there for weeks on end. She pressed a hand to her lips, trying not to cry.

Jack had seen worse grave sites, but he guessed that Rachel probably hadn't. She'd have been better off never having visited the scene. Forever after, in her mind's eye she'd picture her sister in this cold, unforgiving place.

Noticing how tightly she was holding herself in check, he moved closer and turned her to face him. It was one thing to hear of a loved one's death and quite another to visit the scene. Gently, Jack put his arms around her. "Let it out, Rachel. Sooner or later, you've got to let it out."

She didn't want to cry, not in front of this man she scarcely knew. But she couldn't stop the torrent of tears that burst from her, taking her completely by surprise, weakening her knees and shaking her slim frame as she struggled with the onslaught.

Jack held her gently, as a friend might, smoothing her back, soothing her nerves, allowing her the release she'd been needing. He guessed that she hadn't given herself enough time to grieve. He also knew she wanted to be tough, to stay in control. But sometimes, no matter how strong a person was, emotions swamped them and left them helpless. He was certain if his sister had been the one stuffed into that terrible grave, he'd be weeping, as well.

Rachel couldn't have said how long she cried for all the wasted yesterdays and all the canceled tomorrows. She wept for Christina, for her child, wherever the baby was, for her family who'd let Christina down, and finally for herself and the guilt she'd carry forever.

When it was over, she eased back from Jack and found he'd placed a large white handkerchief in her hand. Gratefully, she dried her face and wiped off his leather jacket, which she'd all but drenched. Jack had probably been through scenes such as this before. He seemed to understand, and she was grateful.

Finally she looked up at him, eyes moist and misty. "I'm sorry."

"Don't be. You're entitled." He was unused to women crying in his arms, had acted instinctively when he'd seen her cloud up. He usually didn't get that close to clients.

"Thank you," she answered, pocketing his handkerchief.

His hand on her elbow guided her over to where the police had outlined two separate sets of footprints. Leaning down, Jack examined them carefully. "These over here look as if they've been made by a walking shoe." He pointed to another section. "But those could have been made by a youngster, a teenager maybe."

"Or a woman with a small shoe size," Rachel suggested.

"That's possible." His eyes raised from the shallow grave to the bluff overlooking the canyon and silently he wondered if Christina had fallen down here from up there or been pushed. He needed to see the official report and to read the autopsy report to see if they'd determined exactly how Christina had died.

And what was their best estimate as to what had been used to hit her on the head.

Rachel walked a short distance away, looking around. "Who would want to kill a pregnant young woman?" she conjectured out loud.

Jack strolled over to her. "Why do you suppose she was up here in these hills?"

Feeling cold, Rachel hugged herself. "I couldn't say. If she and I had been in contact more, maybe I'd know what her habits were, such as hiking or whatever. The deputy told me she'd been found in a dress and street shoes, certainly not an outfit intended for hiking."

"But it was August and probably warm."

"Yes, and she loved dresses. She had lovely legs and liked to show them off, so she rarely wore slacks." Narrowing her gaze, she scanned the area. "But what was she doing out here in the wilderness?"

"Maybe meeting her lover, the baby's father?"

"Maybe. But surely they could have found a more comfortable spot. Unless he's a married man and they didn't want to be seen in town." Rachel closed her eyes. "Oh, Lord, I hope that's not the case."

Jack slipped his arm around her, hoping to offer comfort. "We'll find out, don't worry."

"Murder, of all things. Why would someone murder her? Did she know something they were afraid she'd reveal? Had she seen something that would incriminate someone?"

Jack shrugged as he started them on the path back down. "There are lots of reasons for murder. For profit, to cover up another crime, revenge, rage, by accident. Then there are the homicidal ones who kill for sport, or the weirdos who hear voices telling them to kill, or serial killers who murder, for example, blond, blue-eyed women.''

She shot him a look. ''You're full of cheery thoughts.''

''Murder isn't a very cheery thing to have to deal with.''

''No, it certainly isn't.'' Reaching the Lincoln, she waited until Jack unlocked the doors and got in. Wearily, she leaned back against the headrest. This was a lot harder than she'd imagined. But she'd wanted to be involved, so she'd have to manage. ''Where next?''

Jack started the engine, adjusting the heater. ''You said you talked with the deputy, but I have a few questions for him since he's the one who found the body. And maybe the sheriff, if he's around.''

''Fine.'' Rachel closed her eyes and let him drive.

Sloan Ravencrest greeted Rachel warmly and shook hands with Jack. ''Hey, I welcome all the help we can get. As long as you don't keep anything you learn from us and you don't interfere with our investigation.''

''Agreed,'' Jack said, sitting next to Rachel, across the desk from the dark-haired deputy. ''I know you've already told Rachel about finding the body, but if you have the time, I wish you'd go over it for me.''

''Sure. Sheriff Rawlings is out and I have to man the phones, so we might be interrupted, but I'll tell you what I can.'' In his methodical way, Sloan explained how he and Crystal Cobbs had run across Homer Gilmore, an old recluse who lived in the hills, and then followed the trail to Christina's body. Finishing, he looked from one to the other. ''That about sums it up.''

Rachel noticed that Jack never took notes and wondered how he retained everything. He must have a hell of a memory, she decided.

Rising, Sloan walked over to a cabinet, unlocked it and removed a large manila envelope. Opening it, he took out Christina's license plate. ''I can show you this since the lab's finished with it. Only Homer Gilmore's prints were found on it, although there were plenty of smudged ones.''

Silently, Rachel looked at the plate and wished she could turn back time to the first day she'd seen Christina's car with the identifying Chris 37 tag on it, and her standing alongside smiling proudly.

''Then there's this.'' Sloan removed a smaller envelope and let its contents slide onto his desktop. A locket on a broken gold chain slipped out. ''This was found clutched in Christina's hand. Do you recognize it as hers, Rachel?''

Rachel leaned closer, then shook her head. ''No, I don't. But of course, she could have bought it or gotten it as a gift after I left. I never saw her wearing anything like that.''

''Yeah, anything's possible.'' Sloan busied himself putting things back into their evidence envelopes and locking them up.

"I assume the lab's doing DNA testing on Christina?" Jack asked.

"Yes. We found quite a few dried blood spots on and around the body, some hair samples. It's fortunate the killer buried her, preserving things. Also we're lucky it wasn't a rainy fall up there. Might have washed away a lot of evidence." He resumed his seat.

Rachel decided to ask him for a favor. "Sloan, I've been trying to put together a list of Christina's friends for Jack, but I've been gone so long that I really don't know who she hung around with the last few years. Would you know?"

"Yes, especially her men friends," Jack added.

Sloan hesitated, gazing at Rachel a moment, then reached into his desk drawer. "I compiled this off the top of my head, guys I've seen her with or men I've been told knew her." He slid the paper across the desk, toward them.

Rachel tried not to react, but there were more than a dozen names there in Sloan's neat handwriting. She gave him a weak smile. "She got around, I guess." In all her adult life, she hadn't dated that many men, Rachel thought, and she was older than Christina.

Jack glanced at her, then the list again. "I take it you're going to be interviewing these men?" he asked Sloan.

"Right. I've already started. Can't locate a few."

"Do you mind if I talk to them, as well?"

Sloan regarded him a long moment. "All right, I'll give you a copy and mark the ones I've already interviewed. Hold off on the others a day or two. I need to be the first to speak with them. And if you learn anything, call me. Agreed?''

"Yes, sure. Thanks." He waited until Sloan made a copy of the list, marked his choices and handed it to Jack. He rose and offered his hand. "I appreciate all your assistance."

"Hey, we're on the same side here, working toward the same goal," Sloan answered. He walked to the door with them, placing a hand on Rachel's shoulder. "Are you all right?"

"As well as can be expected, Sloan."

"I know it's tough. Hang in there."

Back in the Lincoln again, Rachel examined the list, wondering where to start.

Jack climbed in behind the wheel. "I'm glad Sloan was in, instead of Rawlings. The sheriff might not have been as cooperative. You know, this is a bit of a strange town. You've got eccentrics wandering about, like Homer Gilmore, and psychics with visions, like Winona Cobbs and her niece, Crystal. And, if that's not enough, you've got a sheriff who was supposedly raised by wolves." He shook his head. "Not your normal everyday little Western town."

Even though she'd been gone awhile, Rachel still felt a bit defensive when someone criticized or made fun of her hometown. "Oh, I think all towns have their share of characters. Don't tell me L.A. doesn't. We read in the papers all the time about the kooks you have there."

"You're right about that," Jack said as he started the engine.

A sudden suspicion nagged at Rachel. "How'd you know about Rawlings? From Gina?"

He hesitated, then nodded, again fiddling with the heater's controls. "You know, for the amount they charge to rent this thing, you'd think the heater would work better."

He'd paused a shade too long there, Rachel thought, turning in her seat to study him. Something wasn't right. "You're not telling me everything, are you? Gina didn't tell you about Rawlings. Who did?"

Jack shrugged, annoyed with himself. He was usually more careful. "No one, really."

"Oh, you just happened to *guess* that our sheriff was raised by wolves? Try again, and this time, make it the truth."

He took in an irritated breath. "I checked him out before I came here, okay? No big deal. It's standard operating procedure. I was a homicide detective, remember? Good cops and P.I.'s check out everyone they can before they get involved in a case."

Rachel was getting a bad feeling about this. "Everyone? Like who 'all,' may I ask?"

He let out an exasperated sigh. "The main players. The ones I'd have to deal with. The names Gina gave me of people who might be involved. The sheriff, his deputies, the victim, her family."

Bells went off in Rachel's brain. "The victim's family? You mean you checked out *my* family?" That hadn't occurred to her, though it probably should have.

All right, he'd had enough. It was time Little Miss Tough Stuff grew up. "Yes, *your* family. Your father,

Ellis Montgomery, is fifty-seven, established the Whitehorn Savings and Loan, then went into politics and is currently the mayor though he has his eye on the state legislature. Your mother, Deidre Montgomery, died four years ago at age fifty, from cancer. She came from a prominent Montana family. Had enough?''

''Not by a long shot,'' Rachel said, building up a full head of steam. ''This is fascinating. Go on.''

''Your brother, Max Montgomery, thirty-four, is also highly ambitious, used to travel the globe overseeing the family's extensive investments worth well over a million dollars until he was tapped by Ellis to take over the bank when he was elected mayor. Max lives in a mansion-style home on a hill in the best part of Whitehorn.'' He glanced at her, saw the sparks shooting from her eyes, but he was in too deep to quit now.

''Daughter, Rachel Montgomery, twenty-seven, won a scholarship to the prestigious Chicago Academy of Fine Arts two weeks after she turned eighteen, earned four A's and one B in her senior year finals— not bad. Then she went to work for Kaleidoscope, a well-known graphic arts studio where she's currently assistant head designer. In her senior year at the academy, she met and got engaged to Richard Montrose— an intense but charismatic art student—and moved into his studio apartment. Unfortunately Richard received a grant to study art in Florence, Italy, and bid her a fond farewell two weeks before the wedding.'' He dared look at her again, thinking she'd probably have smoke blowing out of both ears by now. "How am I doing?"

"How could you get all that information so quickly, within a day before you arrived?" Much to her annoyance, her voice cracked.

"It's called connections and the computer, honey." He would have told her in time, Jack reminded himself. She'd forced this confrontation here and now.

"How many others?"

"Everyone I had a name for."

Rachel glared at him, her eyes hot and furious. "You son of a— How could you? You came here, acting all innocent and uninformed, asked me about my family, our friends, and all the time you had all the answers." She didn't think she'd ever felt so angry, so betrayed. At least not since Richard. "You lied to me."

"Never, not once. You didn't ask me if I knew the family's background. Besides, I told you on Day One that I wanted your version of how things went down."

"Lying by omission, an old trick."

"Listen to me, this is a job. Tell me, before you went to work for Kaleidoscope, did you check them out?"

"Yes, but I didn't do a background search on the owner and his wife's private life." She raised her arm, ready to punch him.

Jack saw it coming, grabbed her arm and did what any sane man would do to stop a woman out of control. He kissed her.

And not just a simple kiss, either. He used the arm

he'd grabbed to pull her across the console and into his arms, his mouth taking hers in a fast and furious kiss, since he was as angry as she. Caught off guard, Rachel let out a small sound of protest, but he ground her mouth with his, wanting to get to her, needing to get her to listen and stop overreacting. His other hand slipped up and into her hair, holding her head firmly in place so his mouth could have free reign.

Too stunned to have stopped him, too constrained to break free, Rachel tried moving her head to slip out of his hold, but he held her fast. Just when she thought she might be gaining, her traitorous body began to respond despite her best efforts to stay in control. Suddenly the world seemed to recede, to be very far away, to move into a hazy mist.

She hardly realized when her hands that should have been pushing him away bunched in the soft leather of his jacket and urged him closer, when her mouth softened under his, when her groans of protest became moans of passion. She'd been kissed before, she was certain of it. But not like this. Good Lord, not at all like this.

He was devouring her, consuming her, exhausting her. And the ridiculous part of it was that she was enjoying every second of it. Until the knocking on the passenger window jolted her out of the sensuous fog.

Turning, disoriented, Rachel stared out the window, blinking to clear her vision. It took her several moments to make out Sloan Ravencrest's tall frame. Fumbling, she hit the button to let down the window.

Looking a shade embarrassed, Sloan held up her

leather handbag. "You left this in my office," he told her as he handed it through the window.

"Thanks," Rachel managed to say as she felt her cheeks flame. Whatever must Sloan think of her, necking in the middle of town with a man she'd met only yesterday.

With a final glance at Jack, Sloan walked back inside.

Had that been a smirk on Sloan's face? Rachel wondered as she sank into the deep leather of the seat and groaned out loud. "There goes my reputation in this town, such as it is."

Jack saw that his hands were trembling and hurriedly stuffed them in his jacket pockets. When was the last time a woman had made him tremble? He wasn't certain one ever had.

He cleared his throat. "Hey, it was just a little kiss. What's the problem?" *Just a little kiss. There was the understatement of the year.*

"You obviously don't know small towns."

"Sloan doesn't strike me as a gossip. Besides, you're over the age of consent, and we're both single. What's to tell?"

They apparently lived in different worlds, Rachel decided. Jack thought it perfectly okay to use his connections and computer ability to investigate anyone he wanted to and he saw nothing wrong with necking in broad daylight on a busy public street. He was also the man who'd just turned her mind to mush and her knees to water with just one kiss.

She finally looked over at him and was pleased to see he looked as shaken as she still felt. "Look, I don't think this is going to work. We're on separate wavelengths. Or, as they say today, we're not on the same page. Why don't you bill me for your expenses so far and we'll call it a day?'' What in hell she'd do for an encore, Rachel wasn't sure, but she'd think of something.

''Oh? So you feel eminently qualified to find out what happened to your sister and her baby on your own now?''

A bit of the old anger resurfaced. ''Why not? She's *my* sister.''

''And because the two of you were so close, you know all her friends, her habits, her likes and dislikes, so you can reconstruct her last few months. Even though you were a thousand miles away and the last time you saw her was—correct me if I'm wrong—a year ago come Christmas. And, of course, you've taken into consideration that this person who killed Christina might not want that fact known and if you get too close, he might in fact decide the world would be better off without you, too, right?''

''Damn you!'' Crossing her arms over her chest, she glared straight ahead. ''You aren't the only private investigator, you know.''

''No, but I am the best.'' Gazing in her direction, he flashed her his most charming smile.

''Don't think that works with me.''

''We could try another kiss?''

She shifted away toward the door. ''Back off, bud.'' Rachel sighed, feeling weary to the bone. ''All right, we'll try again, mostly because I don't want to start all over from scratch with some new God's-gift-to-womankind macho man.''

"No, honey," he said, shifting gears, "that was Richard, not me."

That arrow hit the mark. Maybe they were all like that, Rachel decided as the Lincoln pulled away from the curb. "And don't call me honey!"

Three

Matt Hanley pumped gas at the Whitehorn Texaco Station on Route 191 on the outskirts of the city. He was tall and thin, with a feathery dark mustache that didn't go with his dyed-blond hair worn quite long. It was a slow day so he told them he didn't mind answering questions as he strained the back legs of a rickety chair in the cramped little station and lit a cigarette. Some guy from the sheriff's department had already been out, Matt told them. He gave Rachel the impression he was still basking in his fifteen minutes of fame.

He was twenty-one, a year younger than Christina.

He was number four on their checklist of names.

Trying to be open-minded and non-judgmental, Rachel stood back and listened as Jack questioned the boy. She couldn't in all honesty classify him as a man since he looked as if he was just beginning to shave that baby face.

"We were just friends, you know," he told Jack, blowing smoke toward the ceiling. "*Good* friends, if you know what I mean." He smiled, revealing teeth already tobacco-stained. "Christina liked a good time and so do I. I was real sorry to hear she was dead."

He dragged deeply on his unfiltered cigarette and shot a glance toward Rachel.

Ducking the smoke, Jack frowned. "Those things'll kill you," he commented.

"Yeah, well, we all gotta go sometime, you know." Another long drag.

"When did you last see Christina?" Jack asked, wanting to hurry this up. He was fairly certain this young kid wasn't a killer.

Leaning back precariously, Hanley studied the splotchy ceiling, narrowing his brown eyes. "Last spring, we went to a concert in Bozeman. Great weekend."

"Why'd you stop seeing her?"

"I didn't want to quit, man. But Chris, she liked to play the field. She told me that up front. 'Course, I see other chicks, too. Gotta kiss a lot of frogs before you find that princess, you know." Matt grinned at his own garbled joke.

"I suppose so. Did you ever double-date?"

"Nah. I got a souped-up Chevy with a big engine. We liked to go up into the mountains in summer, camp out under the stars, you know. Chris was real smart. She could name all them constellations, the Big Dipper, all that."

Something else she didn't know about her sister, Rachel thought even as she wondered how a beautiful girl like Christina could be interested in this punk. So much for not judging.

"Do you know who else Christina might have been seeing?"

Matt grunted, then grinned. "Lots of guys. She was a party girl."

"Did you know she was pregnant last spring when you went to that concert?"

The chair slammed down on all fours. "Hey, man, you can't pin that one on me. No, sir. If she was knocked up, it wasn't by me. I practice safe sex." He paused briefly, scratched his head. "She sure didn't look pregnant."

Jack was getting fed up with this little creep. "One last question, do you know of anyone special she might have been seeing on a regular basis, say around last Christmas?"

"I didn't keep track of her friends." Moving from chatty to cool, there was relief in his face when a car drove up. "That's it. I gotta get to work."

"Okay, thanks." Jack took Rachel's elbow, guided her back to the Lincoln and inside. Shutting his door, he let out a frustrated sigh. "I think we can cross him off the list."

Rachel stared at the boy pumping gas and flirting with the young girl behind the wheel. "She wasn't very choosy, was she?"

They'd already questioned three others. The first had been Terry Harper, a twenty-nine-year-old divorced insurance salesman and father of two who'd been nervously cooperative, claiming he'd been out of town the week of Christina's disappearance. Next, they'd looked up Rod Calabro, a twenty-four-year-old grocery clerk who fancied himself a top-notch line dancer and said Christina and he used to enter competitions at several area taverns. Though seemingly without ambition, Rod was clean-cut and appeared genuinely sorry about Christina's untimely death.

The third man they'd talked with was Jerry Fisher, a lanky itinerant cowboy who'd worked on several of the nearby ranches and was saving to buy his own spread. He'd answered Jack's questions curtly, his expression impassive. Yet as they were leaving, he confessed that he'd asked Christina to marry him. When Rachel had asked what her sister's reaction had been, Jerry said she'd told him she'd think about it and walked away. He'd never seen her again.

"My gut instinct tells me none of these four had anything to do with her death, but I'm going to check out their alibis all the same. And I imagine Sloan is, too." He turned to study Rachel and saw the sadness on her face. "How do you feel about things so far?"

"Discouraged, disgusted, depressed." She brushed back her hair with two hands and sighed. "I wonder what she was looking for, going out with such an assortment of men. No two alike, yet they all seemed fond of her."

"Some women take more pleasure in the chase than the catch. Maybe she went after these guys, but grew bored with them the minute they were hooked."

"I suppose that's possible. A woman I work with at Kaleidoscope is something like that. In the three years I've known her, I'll bet she's told me about a dozen men she was interested in, yet she's still alone, still on the prowl. It's hard for me to understand that sort of person."

Jack started the car for the heat, but he didn't drive away just yet. "I think I understand. Christina perhaps was like a lot of men. They enjoy the opposite sex, like to have a good time, but basically they don't want marriage, a mortgage, kids, all that.''

Rachel turned to look at him. ''Does that describe you?''

''Probably. Me and thousands of other guys.''

She shook her head. ''I doubt Christina was like that. I think she was searching for something and never found it. Maybe it's tied in with Dad never being around and Max, so much older, not paying much attention to her. I believe she was looking for someone to love her, someone she could make a home with and a family. I never heard her mention wanting kids, yet she had a child.''

''Which could have been an accident.''

''I don't think so. A woman who's been with all those men, she knew how to prevent an unwanted pregnancy. I think she fell in love with her baby's father and something went wrong. If only we could discover who he is. He's the key.''

''We will.'' He glanced at his watch. ''Listen, it's almost five and we haven't eaten since breakfast. You want to try the Hip Hop again? My treat.''

''On the expense account I'm providing, right?''

''You bet.'' He gave her that killer smile and drove away from the service station.

''It sure gets dark early in winter,'' Jack commented, gazing out the picture window of the Hip Hop after finishing a steak sandwich and fries. ''Between the darkness and cold weather, didn't you find it depressing when you lived here?''

"I used to, but I'm not sure the weather was the cause." Rachel finished her glass of milk, which she'd ordered because she'd been having stomach pains much of the day. Undoubtedly due to stress, but she didn't want to add to it by drinking more coffee.

"You were—what, eighteen?—when you last lived here. What would a beautiful young girl have to be depressed about?" He smiled at her, but his question was serious. Rachel puzzled him and he'd always loved solving puzzles.

Rachel toyed with her spoon thoughtfully. Beautiful. She'd certainly never thought of herself as beautiful. Christina was beautiful. Had been, she reminded herself.

"Depression is easy to sink into, if your life isn't all you wish it to be. A job lost, a relationship turned sour, an indifferent family, the dreariness of the long winter ahead, holidays to be faced alone or with people who don't care enough." She'd struggled through it all, both as a teenager in Montana and as a grown woman in Chicago. She'd fought to keep herself from being overcome by those feelings and usually won the battle. But there were times when she'd ached with loneliness, the longing for someone special to love, a family of her own.

Not for the first time in their short acquaintance, Jack wondered if she knew how much her expressive face revealed of her emotions. Rachel Montgomery was far more complex than she appeared at first meeting. "Are you depressed now?"

She forced a smile and was about to answer him when the door to the Hip Hop opened and Winona

Cobbs blew in with a gust of wind, her billowy dress swirling around her ankles. She nodded to Janie and walked slowly to the far booth she usually occupied. Rachel watched her sit and saw Emma Stover, one of the waitresses, hurry over to take her order.

Noticing her distraction, Jack glanced over his shoulder. "What is it?"

"Winona just came in." She met his eyes. "Listen, I know you're beyond skeptical about this woman's visions, but I think we can use any form of help available. I'd like us to go talk with her."

"You think she can help find Christina's baby, don't you?"

"And you think I'm crazy for thinking that. Well, maybe she can and maybe she can't. But I need to try everything available to me."

"All right, let's go." He scooted out of the booth and followed her over.

Winona was stirring cream into her coffee as Rachel approached her. Didn't the woman ever eat solid food? Rachel wondered as she smiled a greeting. "Winona, I'd like you to meet Jack Henderson. He's a private investigator I've hired to try to find my sister's child. Have you got a minute to talk with us?"

"Sit, sit." Winona poured two packets of sugar into her cup, then lifted her bright blue eyes to Jack as the two of them slid into the seat opposite her. "You're a handsome one, aren't you?"

"It's good to meet you, Ms. Cobbs," Jack said, thinking formality might throw her off.

It didn't. "You like Los Angeles? I think it's hot and crowded."

Someone had told her he lived in L.A., Jack told himself. She surely wasn't having visions about him. "It's not hot and crowded here, is it?"

Growing impatient, Rachel cleared her throat to get Winona's attention. "Do you have anything more to tell me about Christina, Winona?"

The old woman's merry eyes turned sad as she dug around in the carpetbag satchel she carried everywhere with her. It took her some time, but finally she pulled out a scarf with several bright colors blended on the silken fabric. "Do you recognize this?"

Rachel shook her head. "Should I?"

"Janie told me that Christina left it behind last summer on one of her visits here." She fingered the soft material, drawing it through her age-marked hands. She closed her eyes a moment, then looked at Rachel. "I hear Christina weeping every time I touch this."

Rachel looked shocked, then blinked back a rush of tears. "Are you sure it's Christina's?" she whispered.

"Yes, very." Winona held out the scarf. "Would you like to have it?"

Rachel reached over, took the scarf and smoothed its silken surface. But she heard nothing, felt no vibes whatsoever, not that she'd expected to. "Is that all you can tell me?" she asked.

"Yes, child. I'm sorry." Winona picked up her cup and sipped.

There was nothing more to say. Rachel thanked the old woman and they said goodbye. Looking neither to the right nor left, she made her way to the door while Jack paid their check. She stepped out into the brisk evening air and took in a deep breath, willing herself to not cry. It had been a very trying day.

Jack exited the Hip Hop and hurried over to the Lincoln, where Rachel was standing waiting. "Are you all right?"

"Terrific." She waited for him to unlock the doors, then climbed in.

Jack walked around the hood slowly, wondering whether or not to put any credence in the old woman's ramblings. He'd never believed in psychics per se, though he supposed there were a few people on the planet that actually could predict things. But for every legitimate one, there were hundreds of fakes. The trouble came in separating them. He knew there were documented cases and many respected people believed in the phenomenon. He just wasn't one of them. He was the doubting Thomas who needed proof.

Taking his seat beside her, he saw she looked beat. "What do you say we call it a day?"

"My thoughts exactly."

"Any place you'd like to go, to relax, unwind?"

Slowly her head turned toward him. "In this town? Let me outline our choices. Other than the Hip Hop, there's Neela's, owned by a Cheyenne chef named Neela Tallbear who claims to have been trained in Paris. They specialize in beef—what a surprise—and the place is usually quite crowded, especially on weekends. The third and final one is the Branding Iron where you can eat or drink, play pool or dance,

Western style, of course. Any of those appeal to you after the day we've had?''

"Not really, but they do sound interesting, for another night.''

"Okay, then, home it is. And if you don't feel like going back to that luxurious suite at the Whitehorn Motel, I can put on a pot of coffee. Or perhaps there's even some liquor in the house. I can say with some assurance that Daddy Dearest won't be home. I don't know where he goes every night—or every day, for that matter—but sometime around midnight, he comes home, goes directly to his room and is gone by early morning. I don't know if he's avoiding me because we disagree about hiring you or if this is his routine even when I'm not here.''

Jack pulled the big Lincoln out of the parking lot, aware she was in an odd mood, probably from the bad taste in her mouth after talking with four men who'd been with her sister and knowing they had ten more to question. He thought he'd try to ease her out of it, although he didn't blame her for feeling lousy.

"Maybe your father's got a lady love somewhere.''

"I'd thought of that. If so, why wouldn't he be squiring her around town, unless she's married or bad news?''

"Maybe he has, when you're not here.''

"Doubtful. You have to know that in Whitehorn, if you sneeze twice within the hour, the news gets around that you have a cold.''

"Oh, it can't be that bad.''

"No? Did you see that older woman at the table across from our booth look at me and shake her head before turning to her grown daughter and whispering something? Or the way Janie grinned and gushed as she showed us to our booth?''

Jack turned onto Sunnyslope Drive. ''I didn't notice the people across from us and I thought Janie was just being friendly. To what do you attribute their actions?''

''The kiss. It's all around town. That sort of news travels fast.'' She'd seen the stares, heard the snickers. Funny to realize she'd never been the object of such attention in Whitehorn before. She had no idea how many of the residents had walked or driven by as she'd clung to Jack in that mindless embrace she was having trouble ignoring, but all it took was one person. They wouldn't soon forget, either.

Of course, she was having a little trouble forgetting that kiss herself.

Funny, she didn't seem the paranoid type. ''If that's the case, these people really need a life. Why would me kissing you be of interest to anyone but you and me?''

Rachel shook her head as he pulled up in front of the Montgomery house. ''I don't know. I only know that, like most small towns, Whitehorn thrives on gossip. And you, being new in town, are especially fair game. And me, living in a dangerous city with mobsters as I've heard them describe Chicago, I'm also fair game.''

Jack turned off the engine and swung around to face her. ''That's truly whacky, you know.''

''Yes, it is, but there you have it.'' She put her hand on the door handle. ''Are you coming in?''

"Are you inviting me?"

He'd turned off the motor so she guessed he wanted to go in. Frankly, she wasn't in much of a mood to be alone tonight, either. She'd be okay, Rachel assured herself, as long as she kept her distance. He was far too attractive and she wasn't nearly as immune as she'd hoped. Still, she could handle him. "Yes, I am."

"Stay right there," he said, getting out. He walked around and opened her door, reaching a hand out to help her. "Just wanted you to know guys in L.A. have manners."

Stepping out, she took his hand. "I don't think manners are regional, but rather inbred." But when he tucked her hand in his big grip and walked close alongside her to the door, she wondered where he'd learned that.

By the time she'd brewed a pot of coffee and carried the tray into the living room, Jack had a roaring fire going. At least tonight she wouldn't have to stare into the fire alone, Rachel thought, pouring coffee. As she turned to sit, she noticed a stack of newspapers on the wing chair. Puzzled as to who'd put them there since she'd last seen them on the hall table, she glanced at Jack and saw him seated at the far end of the couch, patting the seat next to his.

"I promise not to bite," he said.

It wasn't biting she was wary of. The memory of his arms crushing her to his chest roared into the forefront of her mind and she felt heat move into her face. She hoped he'd blame the fire for her suddenly rosy cheeks. Without commenting, she sat at the opposite end of the couch and reached for her coffee.

"Where do you think we should start tomorrow?" she asked him, trying to keep the mood businesslike. She wasn't certain how many more of Christina's old lovers questioning sessions she could handle. But, after all, Jack was the experienced professional who'd investigated a good many such cases. Sooner or later, they'd have to seek out the other men, but she'd let him plan their agenda.

"I'll call Sloan in the morning and see how many others on the list he's questioned. I don't want to step on his toes since we need him as an ally." He drank some coffee and found it hot and strong, just the way he liked it. "Maybe we could visit that hermit, Homer Gilmore. He might be able to tell us something since you say he's always hanging around that area. He could have seen Christina there on other occasions and, if we're lucky, she'd been with some guy Homer recognized."

Rachel slipped off her boots, getting comfortable. "I'm not sure how much information we can get out of Homer. He rambles on and on, not always on the subject. But we can try." She preferred visiting Homer over Christina's ex-lovers.

The warmth of the fire was relaxing her. She leaned back, pulled up her legs and angled her body so she could look at Jack. "So it seems that you know all about my life. Why don't you tell me about yourself?"

"There's not much to tell." Jack set down his cup and leaned back. He looked into Rachel's eyes and could see her determination to know the facts of his life, as he knew hers. "Well, after I left the navy I came home and became a cop. After eight years, I got fed up with that and—"

"Fed up how?"

He shrugged. "With everything. The waste of human life, from poverty, drugs, shootings. The courts try, I guess, but the laws need changing. Smart lawyers for big bucks get criminals off on technicalities and loopholes all the time. I got tired of trying to make a difference. The week before I quit, I was in a dirty alley with a punk who had a switchblade. He'd managed to kick aside my weapon. I thought for sure I was going to buy the farm that day."

"But you didn't. What happened?"

Jack gazed into the fire, seeing the filthy alley, inhaling the stench, remembering the metallic taste of fear in his mouth. "He heard a siren coming closer, my backup. He looked away for a split second and I knew I wouldn't get another chance. I pinned him to the ground, got the knife, cuffed him. I'd had other close calls, but this one, looking into this kid's eyes and seeing that he'd just as soon kill me as not, it meant so little to him. That really got to me." He looked over at Rachel. "He was only fourteen."

Rachel was honestly shocked, even though she'd read about similar accounts in newspapers. "How does a boy that young turn out like that? What happened to him, do you know?"

"Oh, yeah. He didn't spend a night in jail. His lawyer's suit cost more than I made in a month."

"Where does a fourteen-year-old get the money to pay an expensive lawyer?"

"Drugs. You wouldn't believe the amount of drugs in circulation."

"In Chicago, too. I guess that's one reason for living in a rural area like Montana."

"Do you think you'd be happy moving back here?"

Rachel thought about that before answering. "Under the right circumstances."

"Which are?"

A home, a love of her own, a child, a life. "My secret." She wanted to shift the focus back onto him. "What about a woman? Isn't there someone special in your life?" Which, she reminded herself, had nothing at all to do with their investigation. However, the kiss they'd shared somehow made their relationship, although quite new, a bit more personal, so she didn't feel odd asking him.

"Someone special? No, not at the moment. I'm sort of a love-'em-and-leave-'em kind of guy. I'm like my dad that way. He couldn't adjust to marriage and I doubt I ever could."

"You were twelve when he walked out and yet you know he left because he couldn't adjust to marriage?"

"My mother told me repeatedly that he wasn't cut out for wedded bliss. He hated responsibility. He wanted to be free, on his own. I like my freedom, too. I like being on my own, responsible for just me. From age twelve to eighteen, I had a lot on my shoulders, going to school, part-time jobs evenings and weekends, watching out for Gina. Our mother had trouble keeping a job. She had no training. So I took over, way before any kid should have to. I can't tell you how thrilled I was when she remarried and I could let go.''

''You had too much at too early an age. Still, I don't know you very well, but you don't strike me as someone who'd run from responsibility.''

''I don't. I honor my responsibilities. I just don't want to be responsible for other people.''

''I see.'' But she really didn't. Picking up her cup, she sipped and gazed into the fire. He was just another man afraid of obligations, of being tied down. Like Richard had been, needing to be free, on his own.

Rachel felt her stomach muscles tighten. What was wrong with the male population? All of them, afraid of responsibilities, turning their backs on family. Yet most women, herself included, would welcome the responsibility of a child or two, a home, a relationship. Talk about a gender gap.

''Tell me about Richard,'' he asked quietly, for he had a feeling he'd hit a chord with her. Had her ex-fiancé run from the responsibility of marriage at the last minute? Was that why he'd called the wedding off?

She was quiet, thinking, then finally spoke. ''I was twenty-one, in my senior year, and Richard was three years older, a graduate student. Actually I believe a 'perpetual student' describes him better. I imagine he's still studying somewhere. He's very intense, very committed to his art.''

Rachel pictured that lean, asthetic face, the tall, lanky body, his sandy hair worn down to his shoulders, his long-lashed gray eyes. "He was very charismatic, or so it seemed to me at the time. You have to remember that I came from this small town with its solid values and unwritten rules and lines you never crossed. I'd been in Chicago three years and I had some friends, but I was still very green and inexperienced in the ways of the world. Richard was a rebel who lived in a loft, disdainful of rules and regulations, a man who marched to a different drummer—and that's all it took for me to fall for him."

Something struck her as odd. "Now that I think about those days, I believe Christina would have been a better choice for Richard. She had the guts I lacked to thumb her nose at everyone and do exactly as she pleased. I was too much of a coward to do that."

Jack didn't think he should remind her that perhaps Christina's rebellious ways contributed more than a little to her early death. Instead he watched Rachel and listened, letting her talk about her past in her own way, with only an occasional nudge.

"Yet it was you he wanted," he said, intruding on her memories.

"Yes, and I was thrilled. I moved into this really seedy loft with him and couldn't bring myself to tell my parents. I arranged to have my mail forwarded, my calls handled. That should have told me that this alliance wouldn't work, but I wouldn't have listened."

He tried to picture her five years ago living with an artist type in a crowded loft, and had a hard time reconciling that image with the sophisticated, beautifully dressed professional woman he was looking at now. "Were you happy with him?"

"You know, looking back, I realize I was living in a dreamworld. I had visions of helping this poor, starving artist, talented but unrecognized, and one day, he'd be famous and we'd travel and so on. What a fool, eh?"

"No, just young and foolish, not a fool. Youthful indiscretions can be easily forgiven."

"Mmm, I suppose. Richard had no family and no job, so guess who was footing all the bills. I had a very generous allowance, plus I was working part-time. Funny it never occurred to me that he was using me." She shook her head at her own naiveté and picked up her cup, then set it down. She really didn't want more coffee.

"Did he know your family had money?"

"Oh, sure. I told him everything about myself. I suppose if we'd have married, he'd have found a way to get into my trust fund before divorcing me."

"Why did he leave?"

"Because I wasn't enough for him," she answered immediately.

Such a quick reply, as if she'd told herself that very thing over and over. "What does that mean?"

Rachel took in a breath, as if fortifying herself. "We'd set a wedding date, not telling my family."

"Whose idea was that?"

"Richard's, but I went along with it. I thought I could deal with them a lot better after the fact when they couldn't do anything about it. I was over the legal age. Anyhow, I came home from work one evening and found Richard exuberant, dancing all around the place, throwing his few things into his suitcase while he drank cheap wine. It seems he'd received a grant to study in Florence and he was leaving the next day. He told me he was sorry to hurt me, but he really wasn't cut out for marriage. Even with my substantial trust fund, he chose to go. How flattering is that?''

"Come now, Rachel, you must have realized by now how lucky you are that he left. That marriage would have only hurt you more."

"I know that now. I suppose it was mostly my pride that was hurt. You can't imagine how hurtful it is to have someone you'd planned to marry walk away so easily, whistling as he goes.''

"You aren't the first or the last to be left literally at the altar, man or woman. If that's the kind of jerk he was then, he probably still is." He couldn't help himself, he shifted, moving closer, touching the ends of her hair. "He didn't deserve you."

She found a sad smile. "You know the right things to say, don't you?"

"I mean every word. He was a selfish creep. You'd have been miserable. He saved you from a rotten marriage." He shook his head. "I shudder to think how many people would be happier, better off, if they hadn't given in to that urge to marry, which is usually fleeting and temporary.''

An odd viewpoint, Rachel thought. "It sounds as if you've been close a time or two and you're glad you didn't go through with it."

"Actually, I've never been close. I like women and I have a lot of women friends in L.A. But I wouldn't want to spend every day the rest of my life with any of them. I feel that, in order to want to get married, a person should care so much that they can't imagine a world without this person in it. They don't want a day to go by without being with that person. I've never felt that way. I don't think I'm cut out for marriage, so I'm not going to put some poor, trusting woman through all that when I'd probably leave eventually, like my father did.''

She'd watched him throughout that little speech and felt he probably believed every word he said. And maybe he was right.

"If you really want a family," Jack went on, "you'll find someone else. Hell, look at you. You're beautiful, intelligent, funny, feisty. What more could a guy want?" And if she didn't stop staring at him with those big blue eyes, he was going to pull her into another kiss because the last one had really rocked him and he needed to know if that would happen again.

Rachel shook her head. "I don't think so. Being dropped like a hot potato, being made to feel like I lacked something vital, it's not something I ever want to go through again. It hurts too much and the memory stings even years later."

Jack scooted even closer, his one hand on her shoulder now, the fingers of his other trailing the fall of hair that curved along her jaw. "Don't let it. Maybe Christina had the right idea. We should all enjoy life more and worry less." He shifted again, slipping a hand under her bent knees and straightening her legs across his lap so he could gather her closer.

"What are you doing?"

"If you don't know, I must be doing it wrong." He arranged her arms over his shoulders and leaned in to nibble on her silken neck. "Mmm, you smell so good."

"Jack, I don't think this is a good idea." His lips were at her ear now. "Really, I'm serious."

"Being serious brings about premature aging." He touched his mouth to her temple, felt her pulse pounding there.

"Wait! My life is too complicated right now to get involved."

"You'll work it out. An unexamined life isn't worth living." He was moving along her forehead, planting feathery kisses.

Rachel pulled back, surprised. "Socrates? You're quoting me Socrates?"

He sent her a hurt look. "What, you thought I was just some big, dumb cop?"

"No, of course not. But—"

"Tell me, was that kiss we shared in the car so terrible?"

"No, but—"

"No more buts. Does what you felt during that kiss happen with every man you kiss?" He was taking a chance here, but he had a feeling she'd been as overwhelmed as he.

There hadn't been that many men, not since Richard. Though she'd been asked out and even gone several times, she was mostly wary, distrustful. "No, but I don't think—"

"That's good. Don't think." And his mouth took hers, stealing her breath, effectively stopping her protest. But only for a moment as she moved her head aside and squirmed out of his hold, scrambling to her feet.

"Look, I don't want—"

But Jack could be fast, too, rising, grabbing a fistful of her sweater and yanking her back into his arms. He'd never have gone after her if he hadn't seen that edginess in her eyes, the beginnings of passion. He stared hard into those eyes now, but saw no fear or objection, saw instead a challenge.

He'd never been able to resist challenges.

"Maybe, just maybe, you've met your match, lady." Lowering his head, he kissed her hard and deep.

Stunned, Rachel's hands flew up only to be caught between their bodies as he tugged her close against his rock-hard chest. His hands roamed her back, his strong fingers pressing, stroking, coaxing a response. His mouth was the only soft thing about him as he seduced and tempted, his full lips brushing across hers, kissing the corners, then devouring with an ease that was as frightening as it was enticing.

Beneath her palms, she felt his heart pounding as her fingers curled into the soft cashmere of his sweater. She heard a sigh escape as he changed angles and took her deeper, but she wasn't sure which one of them had made the sound. The world became a little blurry as she found herself clinging to him, letting his fascinating flavors tease her tongue as it crept into his mouth.

It was the sign Jack had been waiting for, the assurance that she wanted this as much as he. Arms encircling her, he eased her closer, his response to her nearness instantaneous and obvious. It had been a hell of a long time since a woman had put him on the edge of explosion with just one kiss. The truth was, he hadn't wanted like this in years. But he wanted now.

Without her shoes on, she seemed so much smaller, her bones delicate. She'd risen on tiptoe to better reach him, her slender arms snaking around to settle at his back and pull him ever nearer. She tasted like some fine wine, smooth and sweet, yet with that enticing tingle.

The kiss went on and on, yet was much too short. Finally, Jack released her, fiercely aware that he was getting in way over his head with this woman. He was a man who loved fun and games, the kind that didn't involve feelings. Rachel somehow reached past his firmly planted barricades and touched something inside him. Something he didn't want affected.

He shoved fingers that were none too steady through his hair. ''I'm sorry. I shouldn't have pushed, shouldn't have done that.''

Unnerved at how quickly they'd come so far, Rachel took a step back, then another. Breathing hard, she shook her head to clear it, but it didn't work. ''You didn't do it alone,'' she conceded. There'd been that moment there when he'd looked into her eyes, when she'd known that if she said no, he'd have backed off. But she hadn't stopped him, so she had to share the responsibility.

She made a stab at clearing her throat. "Jack, I don't think this is wise, considering we have to work together."

He braced one hand on the archway leading into the vestibule. "You're probably right."

Surprised that he agreed, she looked up. "Then why are you coming on to me?"

"Because ever since you landed at my feet in that silly bathrobe and those crazy slippers, I've wanted you. I can't seem to stop wanting you." A hard admission to make, but he'd felt the need to be honest. And because now, he knew she felt the same.

His simple statement stopped her in her tracks. Don't make too much of this, she warned herself. Wanting was physical, it wasn't anything more and it certainly didn't involve deep feelings.

Jack pulled his jacket off the coat tree, put it on and dug in his pockets for his keys. "Don't worry. I'm sure we'll get over this, like the flu, you know." He forced his mind back to the case, back to his reason for being in this godforsaken town. "I'll pick you up tomorrow afternoon, okay?"

She should say no, should tell him to go alone, that he could easily handle talking with Homer without her. But she knew Homer, knew how strange and shy he was. Jack might scare him.

She badly needed some time and space to sort out her feelings, to put all this in perspective. The long, sleepless night would have to do. "Yes, okay," she told him.

He left then, without another word, without touching her. With only a long look into her eyes that was enough like a caress to make her heart begin to gallop again.

Rachel locked the door behind him, leaned against it and began berating herself. Why had she let him kiss her? The first time in the car had been unavoidable, so unexpected that it had caught her completely off guard. But this one, she'd seen coming and she'd invited it with open arms. Why hadn't she turned her head, shoved him away? Why?

Because, God help her, she'd wanted to know if the first one had been a fluke, a onetime happening that her imagination had blown out of proportion. And now that she'd found out that each time he kissed her it was like the first time, how could she keep from wanting more?

Four

She'd tried not to think of him, really she had.

After his somewhat hasty departure, Rachel had cleaned up the coffee things, checked all the doors and windows, then gone upstairs. She'd taken a long hot bath where she'd tried to keep her mind uncluttered and free, thinking nothing more complicated than how pleasant it was to lie back amid the bubbles and let her tension dissolve.

Finally in her bed, the same bed she'd spent endless hours during her teen years yearning for she knew not what, she'd struggled to keep her thoughts centered on her sister, the investigation, the missing baby. But just as if she were still that somewhat dreamy-eyed teenager, a tall, handsome image intruded with those green eyes that seemed to look right through her and that killer smile.

Jack had told her in no uncertain terms that he wanted no serious involvement, that he wasn't cut out for marriage. Yet, despite her wariness of men in general and right now, Jack Henderson in particular, deep down inside, she wanted marriage, children and all the trappings. Knowing how he felt and how she felt, she should turn from him, not give another thought to him, certainly not let him touch her again.

Yet even as the thought formed, Rachel knew she probably wouldn't be able to hold firm. For more than five years, she hadn't dated a man more than once or twice, harboring very real concerns about being hurt again. Richard walking away from her practically at the altar had been the single most humiliating experience of her life, leaving an indelible imprint. She was afraid to trust, afraid even to dream that one day someone else would erase those fears forever.

It hadn't been all that difficult, for she'd concentrated on her career, her work. It had paid off; she'd moved up in the company and now, as assistant to the head designer, she was not only in line for that job one day, but she had work she loved, a generous salary, benefits and flexible hours.

Only recently had she begun to think that all work and no play was beginning to make Rachel a pretty dull person.

Rearranging the pillow beneath her head, she settled down again, willing sleep to come. But instead, she relived that last kiss, the one where she'd risen on tiptoe and felt her heart pound in rhythm with his. She'd jumped up from the couch intending to keep him at bay, to send him on his way. Instead, one look, one touch, and she'd opened to him like a desert flower to the first rainfall.

Disgusted with herself, Rachel stared at the ceiling, deliberately coralling her wandering mind. Where was her father? The clock had chimed eleven the last time she'd made a note of the time. Dare she confront him, ask him what kind of meetings lasted this late? Not a good idea, she decided. Ellis would likely tell her it was none of her business, and he'd be right. After all, she didn't want to answer to him so she'd best leave well enough alone. Dad wasn't too happy with her right now, anyhow.

Maybe if she and Jack could discover something, come up with a clue that would lead them to Christina's killer, perhaps then Ellis would come around. She had a feeling that her father had more or less ignored his youngest daughter for years because her behavior embarrassed him and certainly wasn't an asset to his political ambitions. For that matter, he'd pretty much ignored Rachel, as well, and she hadn't given him a moment's worry.

A new thought occurred to Rachel. Ellis might even be concerned that Jack would unearth something about Christina that would bring shame on their family. In his position as mayor, Ellis could strong-arm the police or sheriff's office to bury such evidence. But not an outsider like Jack.

Rachel brushed back her hair and changed positions again. What a mess. Tomorrow she'd have to call Pete Ambrose at Kaleidoscope and request a short leave of absence. Fortunately, she'd recently covered for him on a very large project when he'd had to fly to Florida to settle his mother's estate. She felt sure he wouldn't give her a hard time. She'd pretty well cleared off her desk before leaving.

She wasn't crazy about hanging around here too much longer, but once started, she felt she had to finish. Call it guilt, or belated sibling love, or whatever, she had to learn what had happened to Christina. And then there was the baby.

Rachel hugged herself, wishing the child were here with her now. Would the baby have Christina's huge blue eyes and chestnut hair? Or would he or she resemble the father? And just who was the father? Had Christina been seeing one certain person, someone she loved who'd fathered the baby, or had this been a random pregnancy and the father unknown, even to the mother? She wasn't sure why, but she prayed the child had been born of love.

Her dormant romantic streak, Rachel decided. Well, why not? There wasn't enough romance in the world. Lots of sex, but very little romance and certainly not enough love. The three elements should be in the same package, but were they ever? She had her doubts.

Sighing, she beat down her pillow and closed her eyes, trying desperately to get to sleep.

They were trudging around on the rocky hillside in the area where Christina's car had been found and where Homer Gilmore's shack was located. He'd picked her up around two on a gray and gloomy afternoon that threatened later snow.

"Are you sure we're going in the right direction?" Jack asked, following Rachel up along the trail.

"I'm sure of the general direction, but I've never actually been to his home. I keep hoping we'll run into him wandering around here, which he does frequently."

She'd been very businesslike with him since he'd picked her up, Jack noted. Not cold exactly, but cool and more formal. If it's possible to be formal with someone who's kissed you brainless. "Does he have family somewhere?" he asked, trying to keep their conversation on track so he wouldn't grab her into another mind-blowing kiss.

"I think I remember hearing that he had some family somewhere, but I can't recall the details," Rachel answered, swinging to the right as the path did.

Under her jacket, she was wearing a blue sweater the exact color of her eyes, Jack noticed. Even without sunshine, her hair was shiny and clean, skimming her shoulders as she walked. His hands itched to touch that thick mass, to pull her around to see that quick jolt of surprise jump into her eyes followed by the sudden heat of desire. Like last night.

Instead he dropped his gaze to the path, knowing that if he kept watching her, he'd surely act on his thoughts. The thoughts that had kept him awake a good part of the night.

He'd had her in his arms last night, right where he'd been wanting her, yet he'd been the one to stop, to put the brakes on. Because he'd sensed that Rachel was somehow different than the women he usually spent time with. She had a way of looking at him, quietly studying him, gazing *inside* him, as if wanting to know everything about him.

He couldn't allow that. He'd spent years—while in the service, as a cop and as a private investigator—making sure no woman broke through the careful facade he'd created. He didn't want someone poking around in his past, analyzing him, telling him what was wrong and how she could help fix him.

He liked women, liked their softness, the way their

minds worked, so different from men. But to get tangled up with one forever? That scared the hell out of Jack. He knew he couldn't cut it, as his father before him. He'd wind up hurting her and himself.

And yet...

He watched Rachel stop and peer ahead, perhaps trying to get her bearings out here where every bush looked like every other and the paths were no more than winding, twisting trails often crossing themselves. She was lovely, yet he had a feeling she didn't think so, probably because she'd lived in the shadow of a more beautiful younger sister. A mature man would more quickly be drawn to Rachel than what Jack had seen and heard of Christina, but he didn't think Rachel would realize that.

It was generally accepted around Whitehorn that Christina was a good-time gal. Yet even she must have yearned for a family, otherwise why would an experienced woman such as she have gotten pregnant? As for Rachel, one day in her presence and, despite her wariness because of the way Richard had treated her, Jack knew she was a forever woman. She may be a career woman right now, but with a crook of the right finger, she'd happily settle down in a house with a passel of kids. After all, look how seriously she was searching for a child that wasn't hers.

And, attracted to her though he might be, that wasn't the life Jack wanted. Oh, maybe some part of him yearned for that which he'd never known, the family unit. But he knew himself, knew he'd get bored with that whole scene and want to take off. The responsibilities would crowd in on him and he'd leave.

He couldn't do that to Rachel.

So he'd best not lead her on. If only he could persuade her that they could have a good time together for now, then bid a fond farewell when it was over. He saw her shade her eyes, though there was no sun, and squint through the barren trees, trying to catch a glimpse of the elusive Homer Gilmore. Her hair shifted in the breeze and she shook her head, then turned to look at him.

He wanted her so badly he didn't trust himself to speak.

"I don't see anyone, do you?" Rachel asked, wondering why he was standing a good thirty feet away, quietly staring.

Jack finally found his voice. "No, no one. Maybe we ought to give up on this for today. Don't you know someone who could contact Homer and let him know we want to talk with him?"

"Gosh, if only we had his cell phone number," she answered, deliberately sarcastic. Jack had been distant all morning, seemingly lost in his own thoughts. Perhaps the memory of that stirring kiss was still with him, as it was with her. But they had to move on.

"In case you haven't noticed, there are no phone lines out here, no gas or electricity up this way. Homer roughs it. The only way to contact him is to wait until he wanders into our path. Do you want to give up?"

Jack knew he had to show more enthusiasm. After

all, he was working for her. "Of course not," he said, coming up alongside her. He pulled a pair of small but powerful binoculars out of his pocket. "Let me lead the way and see if I can spot him."

Rachel fell into step behind him. They'd been walking for about fifteen minutes when Jack stopped, gazing through the glasses.

"Here, look through here and tell me if that guy up on that ridge is our man." He handed her his binoculars.

It took Rachel a moment to adjust them to her eyes, then to find the man. "It looks like Homer. He's got long hair and a full beard like Homer has. Must be him since I doubt there'd be two men out here fitting that description."

Keeping his eye on the elderly man, Jack stepped up the pace although the stooped man was hobbling along rather slowly. After several minutes, they were fairly close and the old man heard them. Turning, he stopped, his face registering surprise then fear.

Rachel stepped around Jack and smiled. She didn't know Homer well, but she was sure he knew who she was. "Homer, it's Rachel Montgomery. You remember me?"

Frowning, Homer scratched his bearded chin with a gnarled hand. "You the mayor's daughter?"

"Yes, that's right." They walked closer. "This is Jack, a friend of mine." She held off mentioning Jack was an investigator, thinking the knowledge would frighten Homer. "I wanted to ask you about my sister, Christina. She…she was out here back in late August." It was still difficult for Rachel to envision her sister in these hills, pregnant and in labor, delivering a baby on the hard ground under less than sanitary conditions.

Homer's rheumy eyes glistened with what looked like tears. "Died. She died over yonder." He pointed vaguely in a direction over the next hill.

"Yes, that's right. Were you out here around then? Did you see her or anyone else?"

Leaning on a bent stick he used as a cane, Homer stared off into middle distance, seeing things only he could envision. "Seen her with them white skirts flyin' around in the wind."

Rachel frowned, knowing her sister was found wearing a blue dress. "Are you sure?"

"I done watched her, till she's floatin' up into the sky and done disappeared."

"Sounds like an apparition," Jack said softly to Rachel, then spoke to Homer more loudly. "Was anyone with the woman in white?"

"She be right pretty, floatin' like an angel." Homer smiled.

"Have you seen her since?" Rachel asked, disappointed. The man must have been seeing things.

"Yep. Lots a times. But not for a long while now."

Jack leaned close to Rachel. "I think we're wasting our time with him."

Rachel smiled at the old man. "Thank you, Homer."

Without another word, the old man shuffled off, his gray hair blowing every which way in a sudden strong breeze, his beard reaching almost to his waist.

Jack watched him awhile, then turned to Rachel.

"Maybe he's found some hallucinogens out here in herbal form and brewed himself a happy cocktail. He's seeing visions that are stranger than Winona's."

"Or maybe he's just old, disoriented, perhaps with Alzheimer's." She turned to retrace their steps. So much for help from that quarter.

Taking her arm on the somewhat steep path downward, Jack had to agree. "He wasn't around the murder scene. Did you see how big his feet are? No footprints we saw came even close."

Surprised, she glanced up at him. "Aren't you observant?"

"Just doing my job."

Rachel stopped a moment, thinking. "Maybe Homer actually saw a woman. After all, there's that broken chain and locket found in Christina's hand."

"I suppose that's possible, if you discount the part about her rising into the sky and disappearing."

Rachel had trouble with that part, too. "I know there are some discrepancies in Homer's memory."

"Yeah, you could say that. But what other woman would be up on this hill with Christina? We've been questioning her men friends. Do you know the names of women she was close to?"

"Not really. But I'm going to check with Sloan."

Rachel frowned as she stepped around a fallen branch in the middle of the path.

Jack's fingers laced with hers as he helped her maneuver over the log. His hand was large, solid—much like the man himself was. Rachel knew she should take back her hand and keep touching to only the necessary minimum between them. She knew that when he touched her, she wanted more, which could lead to problems.

But she returned the pressure of his fingers, though she kept her eyes averted. Body signals could speak volumes and, for now, she'd let that be enough. She could enjoy him without thinking of the future. After all, she'd known Jack Henderson only a matter of days. The thing was, she didn't want to include him in her musings because she knew as soon as this case was over for him, he'd leave. He might not walk away whistling, as Richard had, but the effect would be the same. She'd be alone again and hurting. If she didn't allow herself to care beyond a working relationship and a simple friendship, she could protect her vulnerable heart.

That decision made, Rachel felt better. Until she nearly walked into a low-hanging tree branch because her mind was elsewhere, and Jack yanked her out of harm's way and into his embrace.

Startled blue eyes looked into green ones, deep and fathomless. For a very long few seconds she studied how amber specks streaked through the green, how his gaze heated and became intense. Then she pulled free and turned. "Thank you," she said, her voice husky enough to reveal her emotions in turmoil. But at least she'd had the strength to step away from the fire.

She'd taken a few steps down the incline when she realized Jack was not behind her. Turning around, she saw him still standing where she'd left him.

"Are you going to stay here all day?"

He shook his head, but from the look in his eyes,

he was deep in thought. "I have to ask you some-thing. Actually, I have an invitation to convey to you. Would you like to join me for dinner at Gina and Trent's tonight?"

Immediately suspicious, Rachel studied his face and thought he looked sincere. "They specifically in-vited me, or did they invite you and you decided to drag me along?"

"Whoa, there. Man, are you distrustful. The truth is I talked with Gina on the phone last night and she invited *both* of us." He dug his cell phone out of his jacket pocket. "Here, call and ask her if you don't believe me."

"Okay, so I'm a little paranoid…"

"A little?"

"What time?"

"Right about now. She wants to show us around their new house, the baby's room she's fixing up, that sort of thing. Do you want to go or not?" For reasons he didn't want to think about, he wanted to see how she'd interact with his family. But he wasn't about to beg.

Rachel didn't answer until they were both in Jack's car. She would have preferred going back to the Montgomery house and changing clothes, maybe freshening up before going out to dinner because she'd heard the Remmingtons entertained beautifully. But she decided she'd better go as she was since Jack was so impatient. "Sure. I like your sister."

"So do I," he said, pulling away from the curb.

"She and her husband seem very much in love."

"If you believe in such things," he muttered low in his throat.

She heard him and wasn't surprised. Disappointed but not surprised. She was quiet the rest of the short distance, lost in her own jumbled thoughts.

"Here we are," Jack said as he turned into the circular drive of a large ranch-style house.

Looking around, Rachel became aware of the familiar neighborhood. "My brother lives not far from here."

Stepping out, Jack nodded. "Yeah, this is where the monied folk live." His hand at the small of her back, he guided Rachel up three steps and rang the bell. Inside chimes could be heard echoing through the big house. A light snow had begun to fall.

In moments, the door opened and Trent stood there smiling a welcome. "Come on in. Glad you both could make it. Gina's in the study, by the fire."

Rachel noted the huge crystal chandelier shining down on the marble foyer, the winding staircase leading up, carpeted in pale blue, the heavy banister made of mellowed oak. There was an open look about the place with its high ceilings, archways leading into other rooms and long slender windows drawing in the outdoors.

"She started spotting this morning so, on doctor's orders, Gina's to stay put on the couch." Wearing a paisley vest over a white shirt, with black pants, Trent beamed at them. "I'm cooking tonight."

"He's terrific on the barbecue," Jack told Rachel. "I don't know if he can make anything other than steaks."

"Is there anything else worth eating?" asked Trent, a Texan through and through.

Laughing, they entered the study, which was decorated in stark contrast to the beautiful white, gold and blues that Rachel had glimpsed throughout the rest of the lower level. Here was a masculine room complete with huge fieldstone fireplace flanked by bookcases on both sides, a massive oak desk at the far end near a set of three arched windows, and two oversize couches that faced one another in front of the blazing fire. Gina was sitting on one with her feet up, an afghan over her legs.

She smiled a greeting as Jack walked over and kissed her cheek. "How are you feeling?"

"I'm fine. The doctor's just being cautious because of that scare we had a while back." She took Rachel's hand and gave it a squeeze. At her guest's inquisitive look, she said, "I got thrown from a horse early in my pregnancy. But I'm fine. I'm so glad you could come." Her red hair was dazzling in the firelight, her green eyes so like Jack's, sparkling.

"Thank you for inviting me." Rachel glanced around the room. "Your home is lovely."

"I wanted to give you a tour, especially the baby's room, but—"

"We'll wait until next time." Trent leaned down and patted her bulging stomach. "We have to take care of the heir apparent." He smiled at her with so much love, warming Rachel. At least these two gave her hope that it was possible to find real love, even if it had so far passed her by.

"What'll you two have to drink?" Trent asked,

rubbing his hands together, ready to play host. "You name it, we've probably got it. Scotch for you, Jack?"

"Right, on the rocks with a splash."

"Chardonnay, if you have it," Rachel said. A glass of wine might help her relax after the unsettling few days she'd had.

While Trent got their drinks, Jack touched Rachel's hand and indicated they should sit on the couch opposite Gina's. As Trent placed the glasses on the coffee table between the two couches, Gina took a sip of her milk and made a face.

"After this baby's born, I don't intend to drink milk again for a year. Every time I turn around, Trent's shoving a glass of milk in my hand."

"You want a healthy baby?" he asked, his voice teasing as he sat at the far end of the couch and took her feet into his lap.

"Yes, of course, I do. But I've always disliked milk, haven't I, Jack?"

Frowning as if it was difficult to remember, he shook his head. "I don't recall that."

"What? Why, you traitor, you!"

Jack laughed. "All right, so you don't like milk. Mothers have to sacrifice, you know."

"Uh-huh." Gina eyed her husband's drink. "What about fathers?"

"They have to watch over mothers so they do everything the doctor tells them," Trent said.

Rachel listened to the good-natured teasing between husband and wife along with the camaraderie between brother and sister, and found herself envying

Gina. Why couldn't Max be more of a loving brother like Jack was? Would he have been if she'd stayed in Montana? Anyone's guess.

Trent got to his feet. "Ladies, if you'll excuse me, I've got to stoke up the old barbecue. Jack, why don't you come give me a hand? I'm sure these two can entertain themselves while we get dinner going."

"Don't forget the rolls, honey," Gina called after Trent as Jack followed him out. She turned to Rachel and smiled. "How's the investigation going?" She got nightly reports from Jack, but she wanted to hear Rachel's viewpoint.

Rachel leaned back, feeling comfortable with this friendly woman. "Well, we've talked with a lot of people—men who knew Christina well. Nothing but dead ends there so far. Homer Gilmore, who found her car, claims he saw some sort of apparition that night. Not exactly a reliable source." Saddened at the lack of information, Rachel shook her head. "I can't say we've learned a lot."

"Don't give up, Rachel. You'll find the answers, but these things take time. I worked on some cases six months, even more."

Gina seemed so sincere, so genuinely interested that she put Rachel at ease enough to allow her to ask questions. "You really enjoyed investigative work, didn't you?"

"I loved it. Besides, that's how I met Trent."

"Just how did you two meet?"

"Well, it's kind of a long story. Jack sent me to Dallas on this complicated case. Garrett Kincaid's son Larry had seven illegitimate sons and—"

"I'm familiar with the story," Rachel interjected.

"Well, I was on the trail of one of them at the time—that was Trent. He was this big, macho oilman, but utterly charming. I have to tell you, Rachel, he set me on my ear. I went against all my best instincts in getting involved with him."

Rachel got up and took Trent's seat at the foot of Gina's couch since she'd lowered her voice. "Why was that?"

"For one thing, because I knew his reputation with women. He was the love-'em-and-leave-'em type. You've probably known someone like that."

"One or two," Rachel answered dryly.

"Also, there was this rule Jack and I had in the company. Never get involved with anyone under surveillance or who is a part of the investigation. I knew Jack would hit the roof. I also knew if I gave in to my feelings for Trent, he'd still walk away the next day."

This was beginning to sound all too familiar, Rachel thought. "So what did you do?"

"I gave in and went to bed with him." Quickly, she went on to explain, needing Rachel to understand. "I was already in love with him, Rachel, and I simply couldn't help myself. I knew he'd probably leave and I knew my brother would be furious, but I was so attracted that I had to do it. Did you ever feel like that?"

Avoiding the answer, Rachel asked her own question. "And what happened?"

"See, I hadn't told Trent that I was investigating his family. So I turned the tables on him and, after we'd made love that night, I snuck out and went back to California. I guess that had never happened to him before. *He* was the one who always did the leaving. About a month later, Jack sent me here to Whitehorn, following a lead for another of Larry Kincaid's sons. As luck would have it, Trent arrived and I ran into him. He seemed glad to see me and we began seeing each other again. Just when I thought we might actually wind up together, he found out about my investigation. He was furious.''

"I can imagine." Rachel took the first sip of her neglected wine and found it cool and refreshing.

"Things weren't going well, especially when I found out I was pregnant. I didn't want Garrett to find out, or my brother, and certainly not Trent because I didn't want him to feel I was blackmailing him into marriage. So I told no one."

"That couldn't have lasted long."

"It didn't. After a while, Trent learned I was pregnant and he said he wanted to take care of me and the baby, so he proposed. But I turned him down." Noticing the surprise on Rachel's face, she smiled. "Listen, would you want a man to marry you out of a sense of obligation? He'd never once said he loved me."

"Oh, I see. You're right. Then, something must have happened."

"I walked away from him, but then I had the riding accident and almost lost the baby. Trent stayed with me until we were both out of danger. He convinced me that he loved me and the baby and that no one was forcing him to marry me.'' Gina took a deep breath and reached for her milk. ''That's my story.''

''No one who saw the two of you together could mistake the fact that you're very much in love. I admit, I'm envious.''

Gina's green eyes narrowed as she studied the woman sipping her wine. ''How are you getting along with Jack?''

''Fine,'' she answered automatically.

''Really, or are you just saying that?'' She waited until Rachel met her gaze. ''I know he can be difficult.''

''We all can be, I guess. He's good at what he does.'' Including kissing, which he did better than anyone she'd ever known. ''He's funny and charming at times.'' And his very touch could send her into orbit. ''Of course, if you're asking personally not professionally, we've only known one another less than a week.''

''Mmm-hmm. I fell for Trent in less than a day, but not everyone—''

''All right, ladies, time to eat,'' Jack said, coming into the study. ''The chef says we're to go to the table. Gina, let me help you.''

Gina had been watching Rachel's face when her brother walked in and she'd seen her eyes swing to him, noticing that subtle softening that spoke more about Rachel's feelings than any words could have. Accepting Jack's help, Gina walked with them to the kitchen, her busy mind making plans.

Five

Rachel didn't feel the cold on the drive back to her father's house nearly as much as she had on the ride over, despite the snow still coming down, the freezing temperatures and the blowing wind. Undoubtedly that was due in part to the fact that she'd had two glasses of wine over the evening, something she rarely did.

Mmm, but the chardonnay had gone down so smoothly and the steak—something else she didn't eat often—had been thick, juicy, and done to perfection. The whole evening had been lovely with Gina and Trent acting as marvelous hosts and Jack in a fun mood telling stories about his early investigative cases. He'd managed to make himself the butt of several tales, though she doubted he actually had been.

They'd eaten and laughed and had a little more wine. Overall, Rachel couldn't remember the last time she'd enjoyed an evening so much. For those few hours she'd forgotten her problems, her worries over her sister's child, even her semi-estrangement from her father and brother.

And her powerful attraction to the man beside her.

"Are you warm enough?" Jack asked, annoyed at the console between them, wishing for an older model car with a one-piece bench seat so he could coax Ra-

chel closer and at least hold her hand. She'd been
happy at the house, mellowed a bit by wine but certainly not drunk, joining in the conversation, holding
her own even though she didn't know any of them
well. But now she looked pensive, almost sad.

"Yes, thanks, I'm fine." Rachel was sure that Jack
wasn't aware he was the other reason she didn't notice the cold. Just being with him warmed her, chasing away her earlier wariness. What was there about
this man that had her relaxing to the point where she
could hear the walls she'd erected come tumbling
down, brick by brick?

Part of it was that he gave the impression of
strength, of solid comfort, of someone who would be
there for you. What woman didn't want that? And
tonight, watching him with his family, something had
shifted for Rachel in her feelings for Jack. She'd discovered his secret, the one he used to guard his heart
much the same way she'd needed the walls she'd built
to keep herself from being hurt again.

The secret was that inside Jack, so deep inside he'd
probably never acknowledged it himself, he was a
family man. Oh, he'd deny it if she were foolish
enough to give voice to her discovery. But she'd seen
with her own eyes and knew she was right.

No way could he have faked the tenderness he felt
for Gina. It was there every time he helped her do
some small chore, easing her pregnancy. It was there
in the way he looked at her, smiled in her direction,
or touched her hand affectionately. And it was most
evident when he spoke of her baby.

He also liked and admired Trent. Rachel could see

that Jack had taken to Trent like the brother he'd never had. They were on the same wavelength, laughed at the same jokes together and shared a deep love for Gina, each in a different way.

Rachel had spotted something else about Jack that she was fairly certain he'd not acknowledged, and that was his yearning for a home and family much like Gina and Trent had. She'd seen the way he'd sat back at the dinner table, gazing first at his sister and her husband sharing a private moment, then glancing around the room, the house, unaware that his expression was one of longing.

And small wonder after the way he'd been raised, a father who'd left him before he'd entered puberty and a mother who'd been totally overwhelmed by the desertion and had to rely on her very young son to hold the family together. Jack could protest till the cows came home; she'd seen the truth in his eyes. He wanted what his sister had, a loving mate, a solid home, a child on the way.

In other words, he wanted what she wanted.

But wild horses wouldn't get him to admit it, much less act on it.

Rachel suppressed a sigh as she thought about Gina's story which paralleled her own situation: a man who liked the freedom of his single life and a woman who'd fallen for him fast and fiercely. But Gina was beautiful and clever and confident, whereas Rachel had been all but left at the altar once already. That would make anyone a little gun-shy. She felt then and now that she didn't offer enough for a man to abandon his life-style to begin a family with her.

Perhaps she should just enjoy the now and not dwell so much on the future, or the past.

As Jack turned onto Sunnyslope, Rachel saw that her father's vehicle wasn't in the drive. Naturally not, since it was only nine and Ellis usually drifted in around midnight.

Jack stopped the Lincoln in front of the house, slipped it into park and turned to Rachel, a question in his eyes.

Gazing up at him, Rachel knew she could lie to herself and say she should really make him some coffee since they hadn't had any at the Remmingtons'. But, although she could use that as an excuse, the truth was she wanted Jack to come in with her, and it wasn't for coffee.

Maybe it was the story Gina had told her about the way she'd met Trent, how speedily she'd fallen in love with him, and how she'd acted on that fact because she simply couldn't help herself. Almost from the start, Rachel had felt the same about Jack, but she'd pushed aside those feelings, telling herself she couldn't fall in love that quickly.

That was so much rubbish.

There was an old song that said something like "it only takes a moment," and although she wouldn't have believed it before, she knew it was so now.

Still, she had no illusions that her love was returned or that by making love with him, he'd change his mind and stay with her. She'd learned her lesson on that score and learned it well. He'd go when it was over whether she let herself love him or not. And she might be missing the best experience of her life.

She met his eyes honestly. "I'm not going to ask you in for coffee. But I do want you to come in." And she waited.

There was a flicker of acknowledgment of what her invitation implied, a fleeting smile, a change in his eyes. "Good, because I very much want to come in."

"I think Dad has some brandy. You could build a fire." After all, she didn't want to rush things. She wanted to set the mood.

"That would be nice."

Outside, he took her arm and maneuvered them carefully along the walk, slippery with the more than an inch of accumulation, and it was still snowing. On the porch, Jack took her keys and unlocked the door. He let her precede him, then closed the door behind them and helped Rachel remove her jacket. That was when Rachel spotted a note left on the hall table. While he hung up their jackets, she read it.

"Not bad news, I hope," Jack said.

"No, good news, actually. Dad's out of town and won't be back until tomorrow evening." Turning, she looked into his eyes, saw the green darken to emerald, and felt her heart lurch. "I'll go get the brandy," she said, pleased that her voice was steady.

She took her time, looking through the bottles in her father's liquor cabinet, finally choosing a mellow brandy and two snifters, placing them on a teakwood tray. Again, in the kitchen, she paused to check her reflection as she had that first night Jack had entered her life. Was it possible that had been less than a week ago? It seemed as though much more time had passed, as if she'd known him for many months, as if she'd been preparing for this night for a long while.

Rachel fluffed out her hair, noticing that her eyes held a sort of glow of expectancy. She'd chosen the soft sweater that matched her eyes on purpose, believing her eyes to be her best feature, and wondered if Jack had noticed.

Maybe tonight, he'd notice more.

Taking a deep breath and squaring her shoulders, she carried the tray into the living room and set it on the table in front of the couch. Sitting, she watched as Jack piled logs into the grate, his movements as deliberate and controlled as the man himself. He was wearing a black V-necked sweater and black slacks. While she might not see his muscles, she could very well imagine their flexing with each of his movements.

Jack lit a stick of Georgia fatwood, then bent to trail it beneath the stacked chunks, patiently waiting until the logs caught. When he was satisfied, he turned, dusted off his hands, and joined her on the couch, noticing she'd removed her boots and stretched out her legs. She looked relaxed, yet when he met her eyes, he could see an edgy tension there, and thought he knew what was causing it.

She was every bit as nervous as he was.

Silently, Jack poured brandy into both snifters, handed Rachel one before lifting his to his nose and inhaling the potent aroma. Watching her over the rim as she did the same, his eyes smiled into hers, and he felt a connection that had his pulse pounding. He took a generous sip, his gaze still locked with hers, wondering what she was thinking.

She was thinking she didn't need the additional stimulus of the brandy after consuming more than her usual quota of wine. Taking a sip, she felt the heat move down her throat, trail lower and lower, warming her insides. Her cheeks felt flushed. Was it from the brandy or the fire, now crackling and hissing? Or from the man who reached to put both their glasses on the table, then shifted closer to her?

"Turn around," he told her. "You're very tense. Let me see if I can work out the kinks."

Because she thought it would be rude to refuse, Rachel did as he asked, giving him her back, rolling her shoulders. He was right; she was tense. And he'd caused most of it.

"That's good brandy," Jack commented as his hands settled on her slender shoulders, massaging lightly, keeping his touch impersonal.

His voice was as rich as the brandy, as warm as the flames across from them, as exciting as the touch of his hands. "It's probably old, which I guess enhances the flavor. Some things improve with age."

"You will. You'll just get more beautiful."

"You don't have to lie to me. I've been lied to too much." Richard had told her she was beautiful every time he wanted something from her, and never noticed how she looked when he didn't. "I know I'm just average, not stunning like Christina was, nor as lovely as Gina, and I've come to accept that."

"Have you, now? And just who sold you those bill of goods?"

"A number of people." Her mother had been the kindest, saying it would be in Rachel's best interest if she developed her personality and talents, a subtle reminder that she was no beauty. Her father's eyes had fairly glowed every time Christina had come into a room even as a child, but that hadn't happened when Rachel approached him. Max had seemed not to notice either of them. Richard had emphasized how talented she was, her work good enough to exhibit, but he'd rarely given a personal compliment.

Jack's fingers began to dig deeper, to manipulate the bunched muscles, to loosen them. "They were wrong. You mustn't believe your critics. People have their own agendas when they undermine someone else. You have eyes and a mirror. If you can't see beauty there, as I do—and countless others most likely—you need glasses."

Rachel let her head drop forward, allowing his clever hands to work on her neck. "You're just being polite. It isn't necessary." Hadn't she all but invited him into her bed tonight? Why did he think flattery was necessary?

"Are you fishing, Rachel?"

"No," she answered indignantly. "Could we talk about something else, please?" Or not talk at all since she was beginning to feel languid and lazy as her muscles relaxed.

"No, I want to finish this. In my family, Gina got the looks. She's beautiful without question. I got the brawn and the brains."

"Now who's fishing? You know you're attractive, but are you suggesting Gina's not smart?"

"Not at all. I know she's not only intelligent but street-smart. However, I taught her how to survive a fairly bleak childhood by playing mental games. I watched over her when my mother couldn't."

Small wonder they were so close, Rachel thought.

"In your family, from what you've told me, your father apparently got the moxie, Max got the Midas touch, Christina got good looks then squandered them. But you, you got it all and you don't even know it."

What could she say to that? To protest would sound silly, to agree was unthinkable. Instead, she made a purring sound low in her throat. "If you ever want to stop playing cops and robbers, you can take up massaging. You have great hands."

Obviously she wanted to change the subject, which was okay since he was having trouble concentrating. "I haven't wanted to put my hands on a woman like this for a very long time." His fingers trailed to her throat, caressing the silken skin there, feeling her pulse quicken. "You have the most incredible face, the softest skin. I never see you that I don't want to touch you."

She wanted to believe him. Lord, how she wanted to believe him. Languid from the wine and brandy, and the massage, she was too relaxed to notice he was moving to the next plateau. "I thought after I fell at your feet that first evening that you found me pretty amusing."

"In the beginning, maybe." There was a subtle change in his voice, a thickening, as his fingers reached to lazily thread through her hair. "What would you say if I told you I've lain awake these past few nights thinking about you just like this, of being with you, imagining what you wore to bed, what your room was like?''

The same bedroom where she'd lain imagining him. From the first, there'd been that male-female awareness humming just beneath the surface that neither of them could rightfully deny. Rachel felt an electrical tension radiating between them, a seductive energy she was certain Jack felt, too. It was there in the way he looked at her with those hazel-green eyes that seemed to see far more than she intended, in the way his hand lingered overly long each time he touched her. He had a habit of standing a hairbreadth closer than good social manners dictated. She was certain he invaded her space intentionally, hoping for a reaction, and he was rarely disappointed.

Sensing a change in the way he was touching her, she tensed as his hands tangled in her hair, tugging her closer. ''Jack,'' she whispered, startled by the sharp stab of desire the contact aroused in her.

''You make me think of things I'd long ago pushed out of my mind—like a soft summer night and the way your hair smells and moonlight on satin sheets.'' He dipped his head lower and touched his lips to her cheek, the tip of his tongue trailing down to kiss the corners of her mouth. ''Mmm, I love the way you taste.''

''Jack,'' she tried again, knowing the effort was halfhearted, hearing the catch in her voice. ''Maybe we should slow down.'' What was wrong with her? she wondered. She'd never been a tease. She wanted him, had invited him in. Yet suddenly her need for this man frightened her, her own desire overwhelmed her. If he could do so much to her with just his hands and a brushing of lips, what would happen if she gave herself to him completely? "I don't—"

His mouth swallowed the rest of her words as he shifted her in his arms and pulled her up tight against his body.

Passion exploded, immediate, frantic, racing like a speeding bullet through Jack's system. The kisses they'd shared up to now had been but a practice session for this mindless mating call that had him dizzy with need in mere seconds. Seeing her daily since meeting her, trying to ignore the attraction, had only heightened the craving. His arms wound around her, her heart beating against his, Jack let the sensations wash over him.

Emotions swirled then collided inside Rachel, leaving her trembling. His mouth was warm and wet and wonderful, chasing away all rational thought. His dark, masculine flavors burst on her tongue until she was seeped in him, in pleasure. She'd known passion before, but never had she suspected she could feel more, so much more. On a throaty moan, she angled her head and invited him to deepen the kiss, to show her even more, to show her everything.

Outside, the snow came down more heavily, the winter wind slamming gusts against the windows at their back. The fire in front of them spit and sputtered, the logs crackling as the flames devoured them. As if from a great distance, the sound of an owl could be heard, or was it a trick of the wind? Jack saw none of it, heard none of it, as his lips fastened to the pulse point pounding at Rachel's throat. Pounding for him. His hands shifted, moving around front, impatient to touch bare skin. Inching beneath her sweater, his fingers found her breasts, and he heard the moan she couldn't suppress.

Rachel's heart beat like a captive bird beneath his hand as he caressed her quivering flesh, then dipped his head to taste. Her hands moved into his hair and pressed him closer as he suckled her, then shifted to swallow her cries. Their mouths locked in fiery demand, in frantic need. They rolled together on the outsize couch, breathless and panting.

Jack was stunned to his core, unable to function beyond holding her, caressing her. Needs whipped at him, making his mind hazy. He wanted her desperately, to love her all night long. But not here in this living room on the couch where Ellis could possibly arrive home from a change in plans and find them. Breathing hard, he eased back a fraction.

Through a brain still cloudy, Rachel struggled to catch her breath, to think clearly, to make sense of what was happening here. A hurricane, an avalanche, a tidal wave or something no less forceful. Never in her wildest dreams had she thought she'd feel so much.

Did he feel the same? Did he want to go upstairs to her room to finish what they'd started? Or did he want to leave, to give them time to think this over? She needed to know. Taking in a deep breath, she moved back and looked into his eyes.

She saw her answer there in the emerald-green

depths. He wanted her as no one else had ever wanted her before. Rising, without a word, she took his hand and led him up the stairs.

Peripherally, he saw that her bedroom was large, decorated in shades of yellow and white, with a big double bed and a door that led to a private bath. He stood still, watching as she cautiously locked the hall door, then walked over to light a chunky candle on her nightstand and another larger one on the dresser. The flickering candles lending their pale light, he could see, through the filmy curtains of twin windows, the snow continue to fall.

So she liked romantic trappings, subtlety and privacy. He would give her romance tonight and unlock the passion inside her that would prove to her how beautiful he thought her to be. He held out his arms, giving her one final choice.

Without hesitation, Rachel stepped into them, offering her mouth.

Jack kissed her slowly, gently, keeping himself in check, knowing he'd have to pace himself. Unhurried, they rained kisses on each other, lips trailing along faces and necks as candlelight flickered and snow blanketed the outside world.

Again, she stepped back and met his eyes. "I want a shower," she said. "Will you take one with me?"

"I'm game if you are," he answered, thinking it wouldn't hurt to slow down a little here. Showering with someone was a first for Jack, but he was a willing pupil as he watched her tug off her sweater and toss it onto a chair. Because he wasn't moving, she went to him and touched her mouth to the bare skin revealed in the vee of his sweater. He felt her lips caress there, then her tongue dance over his heated flesh. Stepping back, her eyes on his, she took hold of the hem of his sweater and pulled it over his head, tossing it alongside hers.

"I've never undressed a man, but if you're not going to help, you leave me no choice," she said, her lips twitchy with nerves. Never had she been so bold, Rachel thought, wondering if it was the wine or the talk she'd had with Gina. Or perhaps it was her own unbridled desire.

Jack stood silent, watching her, a challenge in his eyes.

Accepting, she smiled and touched her hands to his belt. Her fingers were trembling yet surprisingly cool as they went to work and in minutes, he wore only navy briefs. She knew better than to keep going, so instead she tugged off her leggings before heading into the bath and turning on the shower.

Rachel sensed rather than saw him follow her as she adjusted the temperature of the water. When it was just right, she slipped off her underthings and stepped into the tub.

His heated blood churned as needs clawed at Jack. He removed his briefs and got in with her, telling himself to take it slow, to savor, to enjoy.

She fit into his arms, he found himself thinking as he molded her soft body to his, her frame small and delicate, her head coming just to his chin. But he'd watched Rachel all evening, smiling, talking with Gina, laughing, and his desire for her had only escalated as he'd realized how well she fit with his family, too. Not that he'd been searching for someone to fit in, but if he had, Rachel would be the one.

The steamy water sprayed down on them as Jack bent to kiss her. Her mouth so warm, so giving, and her hands at his back so arousing as they caressed him.

After a moment, she broke away to reach behind her for a bath sponge. Squirting liquid soap into its center, she tossed her head in a vain effort to tame her wet hair before turning back to him. Her face serious now, she worked up a lather on the hair of his chest, then splayed her fingers there, massaging and stroking. She felt his arms go around her to steady them both, then saw him close his eyes as her hands spread fragrant soap bubbles across his shoulders and along his arms. Turning him, she went to work on his back.

After what felt like interminable minutes of exquisite torture, Jack had a burning need to take over. He placed both his hands over hers at his sides, capturing the sponge. Pulling her body close up against his back, he held her there, moving slightly, wet skin slip-sliding over wet skin, the gentle motion highly erotic. Turning to face her, he squeezed lather from the sponge onto his hands then trailed the soapy bubbles across her shoulders, and along her arms, stopping at her breasts.

Again his mouth returned to crush hers, to drink from her. She was losing ground fast, Rachel thought as her fingers moved up to clench in his thick, wet hair. Rachel sucked in a stunned breath as he lifted her easily, bringing her breasts to his waiting mouth.

He pulled on her slowly, thoroughly, and she was lost, drowning in sensation as she wrapped her legs around his waist. There was no mistaking the depth of his arousal. Her breathing erratic, all she could do was hold on.

His big, gentle hands roamed her back as, with teeth and tongue, he tormented her—and himself—driven by a kind of frenzied passion, the longing to possess her completely shocking him as never before. He let her legs slide down his body, then backed her up against the slick wall as the water thundered down on them.

His hands raced over her, followed by his seeking mouth as her head fell backward and a deep moan came from between her parted lips. When his fingers found her and slipped inside, he felt her knees nearly buckle as she labored to stay upright.

Tossed about on a sea of sensation, Rachel experienced passion so intense it stunned her. She let him lead her, let him take her, then cried out his name before going limp in his arms. Several moments later, her breathing ragged, she met his dark green gaze.

"I wanted to go slowly," Jack confessed, his voice thick and ragged, "but with you, I can't seem to."

"Then don't," she whispered huskily.

Lifting her again, he leaned her against the wall and lazily brushed his lips against hers, back and forth, over and around, until Rachel lost all patience. Shifting, she took hold of him and guided him inside her.

His hands cradled her, shifting her weight until they were deeply joined. With her arms draped over his shoulders, he began to move. The time for slow loving was past. The rhythm was wild, both of them impatient and needy.

Jolted by the depth of his craving for this woman, Jack watched her beautiful face as she strained with him. Finally he felt rather than heard her astonished cry join his own as they trembled on the precipice for a long, brilliant moment, then went over together.

Struggling to keep them both upright, he adjusted their positions and leaned against the tile wall, holding Rachel close in his arms. Burying his face in her wet hair, he let the sweet waves of pleasure roll over him.

Long minutes passed before Rachel felt able to move. Finally, she found her footing and shoved her wet hair off her face with both hands. She felt a shade awkward and somewhat embarrassed at how anxious she'd been, how willing and eager. She was dying to know what he was thinking as she looked into those fathomless green eyes. *Be cool,* she told herself. "I— I hope I didn't hurt you," she said, her lips twitching.

He smiled then and his eyes warmed. "Just a little, but I heal fast."

She'd never been good at pillow talk, never knew what to say. Here, in the shower, she couldn't exactly pretend fatigue, roll over and try to sleep. She decided to let instinct guide her and prayed she wouldn't get hurt by leading with her feelings.

She lowered her gaze to his chest where her fingers swirled the dark hairs there. Searching for the right words, she shivered and felt Jack reach over to turn off the water that had begun to cool. Finally, she looked up into green eyes watching her intently. "I—I honestly didn't know it could be like this," she said, her voice scarcely a whisper.

Touched by what she said, her sincerity, he answered in kind. "I have a feeling that what happened between us just now doesn't happen all that often. With just anyone, I mean." *Careful,* he warned himself. *Don't get in too deep.*

"I suppose not." It certainly hadn't for her, not that she was vastly experienced. Had it been because she'd been so needy? Was he just being polite because he didn't want to upset her?

There was a lot going on in that beautiful head of hers, Jack thought, but this time he couldn't read her expression all that well. So he pulled back the shower curtain, stepped out and grabbed a towel. Wrapping it around his body, he anchored it at his waist, then grabbed another and held out his hand to her.

Rachel got out of the tub and let him envelop her in a big, fluffy towel. As she stood with her back to him, he gently patted her dry while she closed her eyes and let him. What she hadn't been prepared for was when he picked her up and carried her out of the bathroom.

Alongside the bed, holding her comfortably in his arms, he studied her lovely face. "What are you thinking?"

"That no man has ever held me like this before." The blue of her eyes deepened. "I like it." He made her feel small, feminine, fragile.

"I'd like to give you a lot of firsts."

"You already have." But she didn't want to enumerate them right now, sure he would think her very small-town.

"There's more." He laid her on the bed and followed her down.

"We have all night." He was here, in her bed, where she'd pictured him every night since meeting him. She felt her heart pick up its beat as her hand trailed along the edge of the towel knotted at his waist.

"No, not this time," he said, stopping her hand. "This time we go slowly." He would hold back and savor, for her. He would make love to her as she deserved to be loved, with reverence, with feeling. In the shower, they'd been wild and hungry, hands and mouths seeking, impatient, their need huge. His hunger was no less now, reawakened already, but he wanted to cherish her, to let her know how lovely she was, to convince her with his lovemaking what he couldn't put into words.

"It isn't necessary," Rachel whispered. As long as he wanted her, that was all that mattered.

"Yes, it is." Jack leaned down to her, one elbow braced on the bed, his hand stroking her hair, his eyes filled with wonder, as if it were the first time he was seeing her. "So beautiful. Even when we're not together, I see you. At night, I close my eyes and you're there."

She was having trouble believing him. "You never said a word…"

"I know. I'm not good with words."

Her lips curved into a smile. "You're doing just fine."

Easing back, he opened the towel he'd wrapped her in and let his eyes feast on her. With one fingertip, he traced the fullness of her breasts, slowly, gently. He saw color move into her face as her body reacted. His fingers glided as if over something precious, something priceless.

When he put his mouth to her, Rachel arched and shut her eyes as vivid colors exploded behind her closed lids. "I've never wanted like this. Never." She had to tell him, to let him know. Perhaps it wasn't smart, but she couldn't keep her feelings locked inside. "Only with you."

Jack could give her no answer except to frame her lovely face with both hands and capture her willing mouth. Slowly, making her ache with the waiting, he eased his hands into her hair, thrusting through the damp strands and massaging her sensitive scalp with long, lingering strokes, much as he'd done to her shoulders earlier. "You make me crazy, Rachel. You take away my concentration. Why is that, you suppose?" His voice was hoarse to his own ears.

Steeped in him, in the way his hands and lips moved over her, she had no breath left to answer as his mouth closed over the peak of one aroused breast. Unable to lie still, she shifted, shoving her hands into his hair, as he pleasured her until she was arching and straining.

Rachel felt delirium closing in on her. No one had ever made love to her with such infinite care, with such tenderness, each touch whisper-soft, as if her needs were all that mattered. She sighed his name as she reached for him.

"Not just yet," Jack said. Kneeling over her, he sent his hands on a lazy journey, acquainting himself with her lovely limbs. His open palms caressed every inch of her sleek arms, her flat, quivering stomach, her incredibly long legs.

Eyes on her face, he skimmed his hands down one leg, then the other, along her rib cage slowly, then picking up speed. Over and over until he had her squirming, thrashing. He knew the moment she stopped feeling vulnerable and gave herself willingly over to him, letting him take her where he would. At last he trailed his fingers up the inside of her thigh and closed over her. He watched her arch as he sent her soaring, felt her heat pour into his hand and wanted to cry out at the passionate way she responded with wholehearted abandon.

Not giving her time to recover, he put his mouth to her, into the fire. In seconds, a sound very much like a sob escaped from between her parted lips. Finally, she shuddered and curled into his arms.

He'd begun this for her pleasure, Jack reminded himself, but he was the real winner. He'd wanted to reach her as no man ever had before, and instead, he'd found a craving, a longing such as he'd never known before. The seducer had become seduced, he thought with no small amount of surprise.

Naked and damp, Rachel lay with muscles quivering, trying to catch her breath. Surrender was a new word to her vocabulary, one she'd thought she'd never apply to herself. But surrender she had, to his way, to his lead, to her own unleashed desire. She was shaken to the core, to the point of no longer being able to hide it or care if it showed.

Jack stood and removed the towel from his waist.

He was a gorgeous specimen wearing only candle-light, Rachel thought. Long and lean and tan, hard and strong, as close to male perfection as she'd ever seen. Incredibly, she wanted more and reached for him. His eyes darkened as he slipped into her as nat-urally as if they'd been lovers for years. She kept her gaze locked with his as he filled her, as the heat built and built inside her. She knew he'd held off as long as he possibly could, that slow loving was what he'd intended, but his control was shattering. She took pleasure in knowing she was the one who'd brought him to the brink.

Rachel saw his need take over as he drove himself into her mindlessly, glorying in seeing him this way, his dark desire and his hunger a living thing, pushing him on. Her hands bunched on his back as she rode with him, as the heat engulfed them both.

At last, she arched upward, straining to hold in the pleasure just a little longer. But she lost the battle and let go of the room, of reality.

Blood rushed like a thundering waterfall through Jack's system, hot and dark and insistent as he neared the summit. His vision blurred, his heart all but burst-ing free as he finally emptied himself into her.

"I'm crushing you," Jack said some moments later, too comfortable to want to move, but aware that his weight was heavy on her.

"No, it's all right. I think you've killed me so it

really doesn't matter if you get up or not." Rachel let out a long, contented sigh. With a great deal of effort, she overcame the marvelous lethargy and raised a hand to her hair, which must look a sight after being soaked by the shower, followed by the ravishing.

Ravishing, she thought, smiling. What a wonderful word.

"You don't look dead," Jack said, placing a kiss on her ear and rolling over. "You look wonderful."

"Oh, I'm sure."

He reached to take her hand as she tried to finger-comb her hair. "It's the truth. A woman is at her most beautiful after being thoroughly and completely loved."

And that she had been, no question. Her smile widened as she looked at him. "You don't look half bad yourself. Does that apply to men, too?"

"You bet." He smiled, then stifled a yawn. "I should get going, eh?"

She hesitated, hoping she was doing the right thing. "You don't have to. I'd like you to stay the night. That is, if you want to." She tried not to sound desperate or coaxing, but casual and inviting.

He moved back to nuzzle her. "I'd like to stay, but I don't know when your dad will be back."

"Probably not early. Besides, I'm not a teenager." Although she'd felt a few qualms about taking a man into her childhood bedroom. She was positive Dad wouldn't approve, most especially since the man in question was the P.I. he didn't want around. However, if he came home and found them together, so be it.

She was a big girl now and if he gave her a hard time, she'd move out until Christina's investigation was over.

"Then maybe we should get more comfortable." Jack got up and they both rearranged the bedcovers, then crawled under.

Rachel turned onto her side and he curled against her back, spoon style. Breathing a sigh of contentment, she wondered when if ever she'd felt this wonderful.

"I just need a little rest before we start Round Three," Jack said, his voice half teasing, half serious.

"Round Three?"

"Yeah, you think you can keep up?"

"I'll give it my best shot," she said, smiling. "Oh, damn, I forgot the candles." Yet she hesitated, unwilling to dash around in front of him without her clothes, despite what had just happened.

"I'll put them out." Jack crawled out and went to the dresser. He'd no sooner blown out that candle when they both heard the doorbell, two long blasts. Surprised, he looked at Rachel, then the nightstand clock.

It was nearly midnight.

Six

"Who on earth could that be at this hour?" Rachel asked, shoving back the covers.

Jack heard a sound and went to the front window to look out. "Looks like whoever it was changed their minds. A car just drove off."

Rachel finished tying the belt of her robe. Not the ratty chenille but a soft pale blue terry she'd brought from home. Quickly she ran her brush through her hair on fleeting thought that it might be Ellis home early, being dropped off by a friend because he'd had too much to drink and couldn't find his key. If he saw her like this, her lips swollen from Jack's kisses, her face with the unmistakable glow of being well loved, he'd likely throw them both out. He'd have to be truly drunk to miss the signs.

"I think I'd better go see," she told Jack, bracing herself for a scene. "I'll be right back."

Grabbing his pants, Jack shoved a leg in. "I'm not letting you go down there alone this late at night."

"Don't be silly," Rachel said, unlocking the bedroom door. "This is Whitehorn not L.A. or Chicago."

Zipping up, he slipped his bare feet into his shoes. "Need I remind you that your sister was killed here in Whitehorn?"

That sobered Rachel. She hadn't been thinking along those lines. "I didn't think killers bothered to ring the doorbell," she commented dryly.

Rachel hurried downstairs, Jack close behind her. She slipped back the dead bolt on the front door and reached for the knob, but Jack stopped her.

"Let me," he said, his voice firm.

There was no point in being foolishly brave, Rachel thought, and stepped back, praying her father wasn't out there. However, Jack was the one with experience, the former cop. Better to be safe than sorry.

When he first opened the door, Jack didn't see anything or anyone. Then he glanced down and saw a brown basket on the porch near the door, a thick blanket inside. There were footprints in the snow, one set leading from the curb to the basket another back.

"What is it?" Rachel asked from inside the doorway.

Jack bent and picked up the basket, turning back inside with it. "Just this," he said, holding it by its curved handle.

"You couldn't see anyone?" Rachel wanted to know.

Suddenly the blanket began to shift in fluttery little movements. Jack's suspicious mind leaped ahead and he wondered if he was right as he shoved the door closed and carried the basket into the living room where the lamp was still burning and the remnants of the fire still glowing. He set the basket down on the hearth and opened the blanket.

"Oh!" Rachel said, shocked. "It's a baby!"

His guess had been right, Jack thought.

Elbowing him aside, Rachel moved closer, noticing that the child was wearing a long drawstring nightie, a sweater that looked hand-knit and a matching little pink cap. From the edges of the cap, tendrils of straight black hair escaped and clung to the child's round face. As Rachel reached to stroke the soft cheek, the baby opened eyes as bright a blue as a cloudless Montana sky.

Rachel gasped out loud. "I'd recognize those eyes anywhere. This is Christina's baby." Carefully she lifted the child from the basket and walked over to the couch where she sat to take a better look.

"Are you sure?" Jack asked, bracing a hip on the coffee table where their forgotten brandy glasses rested. His suspicions well-founded, still he needed some proof. "There's no mistaking this baby has Native American blood." The straight dark hair and features were a giveaway.

Slipping off a tiny hand-knit bootie, Rachel gazed at the sole of the baby's right foot, then smiled. "There it is, the same birthmark Christina had, a reddish crescent moon just above the arch. We all have the same one. Max, too."

The child didn't seem to mind that two strangers were staring and poking around while her solemn blue eyes studied them. The baby didn't make a sound as Rachel took off the cap and checked the diaper.

"A girl." Rachel felt a rush of emotion flood her. "Isn't she beautiful?"

Jack was busily checking the contents of the deep basket. "We have half a dozen cloth diapers, three bottles of milk, two little nighties the same as she's wearing." He studied the garments closely. "These aren't from a store. They're handmade, hand-embroidered."

"Who made you those lovely little things?" Rachel asked the baby and was rewarded with a spontaneous smile. "Oh, look, she smiled."

But Jack was looking at something else. "There's a note in here with your name on it." He handed it over.

Rachel read it out loud. "'Rachel, please take care of my baby, Alyssa. I'll be back for her as soon as I'm able. I'm her father and I love her very much.'" She checked both sides of the single sheet of paper. "No signature."

"I'm going to check outside. Maybe he stuck around to make sure you heard the doorbell and took her in." He went to pull on his jacket. "After all, it's cold and snowing."

The deaf could have heard that doorbell, Rachel thought as she rewrapped the baby in the blanket. He'd apparently seen the car out front, the car in the drive, the lights on, and figured someone was home.

"Alyssa. What a pretty name you have." Adjusting the child in her arms, she rose and walked around the living room, humming softly. The baby wasn't wet and she didn't appear hungry. Hopefully, she'd go to sleep so Rachel could make plans.

Calculating, she decided Alyssa had to be about three months old. Babies that age slept through the night, didn't they?

In a gust of swirling snow, Jack came back in and locked the door. He rubbed his cold hands together.

"No one around, and the footprints only lead to the curb." Large footprints, probably made by a boot. A big man's boot. "Damn, I wish I'd gone to the window sooner and gotten a better look at that car."

But Rachel didn't really care who'd dropped off the child as she cuddled her close and saw those lovely blue eyes grow heavy.

Jack stood watching Rachel with the baby, an unmistakable maternal glow on her face. She looked like Gina did whenever his sister talked about the child she would have. What was it about babies that instantly changed a woman into a mother, even when they hadn't given birth to the one they're holding? Not every woman, of course. His own mother was far from motherly, a helpless female who liked being taken care of rather than being the one to give the care.

"So, now what?" he asked Rachel.

"Tomorrow, I'll go out and get some things. Formula, diapers, clothes, a portable bed. She'll outgrow that basket in no time. I'll keep her in my room. Oh, and a baby book." What she didn't know about babies would fill volumes. But she would learn.

She was making long-range plans already, Jack noticed. He hoped she wouldn't get hurt if the baby's father came back in a couple of days. "Do you think you should have a doctor check her out?"

"I will, although she looks perfectly healthy to me." Rachel wasn't certain she wanted the news that she had Christina's baby spread around town just yet, although she supposed there was no avoiding it.

"From the way he wrote that note, her father wanted to be sure I knew this was his child."

"Maybe Christina told him to take her baby to you if something happened to her."

"Maybe, but back in August, I was in Chicago with no plans to return. I wonder why he had to leave her."

"And I wonder who he is." Jack took off his jacket and hung it up. "We should go over to the Laughing Horse Reservation and talk with someone at the tribal office. The Bureau of Indian Affairs must have a representative there. Maybe someone saw a man who lives on the reservation trying to raise a baby alone and having a difficult time of it."

"You can try, but from what I've heard, you won't get much cooperation." Resuming her humming, Rachel saw that Alyssa was asleep, obviously comfortable in her arms. And, oh, how she loved holding her.

Jack noticed that Rachel had said that *he* could go talk to them, not *they* could go. "Are you abandoning the search for your sister's killer now that you've got her baby?"

"No, of course not. I just may not be able to be a hands-on participant every minute. I have to take care of Alyssa. But we can meet to map out strategy and you can come over each evening so we can go over what you found out." She nuzzled the sleeping child. "I just don't feel comfortable leaving her with anyone just yet."

Jack yawned behind his hand. "Maybe we should get some sleep and continue this in the morning."

"Good idea. Bring the basket, will you?" she

climbed the stairs to her room. Again, she locked the door and settled the baby in the basket, then placed it alongside the bed. She stood gazing down at the child, her heart full.

"It didn't take you long to fall for her," Jack commented, slipping his arms around her and easing her back against his body.

"What's not to love? She's beautiful and trusting and vulnerable. And she's got my family's blood." She turned in his arms and looked up at him. "Tell me you could walk away from that—and remember that I've seen you with Gina. If, for some reason, Gina's baby needed you, what would you do?"

"I'm going to take the Fifth on that. I can't be responsible for statements made in the middle of the night in the heat of passion."

"What passion? We're just standing here."

Jack's smile was devilish as he ran a hand along her spine, pressing her lower body intimately to his. "Not for long."

Willingly, happily, Rachel went back to bed with him and this time, at least for her, there was a depth, a poignancy to their lovemaking that she hadn't noticed before. Was it because the addition of Alyssa to her life gave her a sense of completion she hadn't had before? Or was it that each time she and Jack made love, she discovered new and wondrous feelings?

Yet later, as she lay curled in his arms, her lover sleeping in the soft glow of a night-light near Alyssa's basket, Rachel faced some harsh truths. The note had said Alyssa's father would be back, which meant she had the baby only temporarily. Of course, he could change his mind, or circumstances could keep him from returning. Especially if he turned out to be the one who'd murdered Christina.

Oh, Lord, could a man kill the woman who'd just given birth to his baby? Could he take that baby and lovingly care for her for three months before giving her to someone he felt would not abandon her? How did he know that she'd be good to his daughter? What had Christina told him about her sister? Was the father someone Rachel knew? She was acquainted with several Native Americans both on and off the reservation, but not close friends with any one of them. Yet apparently Christina had been.

Another thought intruded, the return of Ellis tomorrow. Her father had made it clear on many occasions how he felt about ''Indians.'' He thought they should stay with their own kind and that interracial relationships should be outlawed. What was he going to say when he realized that an Indian had fathered his daughter's child? Rachel shuddered at the thought.

Jack stirred in his sleep, edging her closer to his warm body. How good it felt to be in his arms. Yet the difficult truth was that eventually she'd mostly likely lose him, too. So both Alyssa and Jack would be gone from her life. She'd fallen in love with both in an instant, but that love probably wouldn't be enough. She'd been through this before, and it didn't get any easier. She'd tried to guard her heart against that kind of pain, but it hadn't worked out that way.

Rachel let out a ragged sigh. The best she could do at this point was to make the most of her time with both Jack and Alyssa. And hope for the best.

* * *

"You're kidding!" Gina said, looking into her brother's eyes. "You're *not* kidding. The father left the baby with Rachel? And how does she feel about all this?" Seated across from Jack at the Hip Hop Café, Gina took a bite of her English muffin.

Jack had called this morning and asked her to meet him for breakfast, that he wanted to run a couple things by her. It was something they'd done a lot when she'd been his partner. These morning sessions where they compared notes on their cases and brainstormed had been the most productive. Since her marriage, Gina had felt somewhat out of the loop and was tickled when Jack had called her, especially since she knew the people involved.

She'd arrived well before Jack and had sipped on another endless glass of milk, eavesdropping on the folks around her, especially a seedy-looking biker couple at an opposite table. Old P.I. habits died hard, she guessed. Good thing, since technically she still had a case—finding the missing seventh Kincaid grandchild.

"Rachel's nuts about Alyssa already," Jack answered.

"Alyssa. Pretty name. Does she look like Christina?"

"Her features are Native American and she's got straight black hair, but her eyes are big and blue. Rachel says Christina had the same eyes. And she has a birthmark that apparently all the Montgomerys have, a crescent moon on the sole of the right foot." Which was where he'd started nuzzling on Rachel this morning, working his way up her supple body, taking her from languid to loving in minutes. With difficulty, Jack brought his attention back to Gina.

Gina's shrewd gaze stayed on his face. "Hey, big brother, why the faraway look? Is Rachel getting to you?"

He frowned, annoyed she could see through him so readily. "I didn't get a lot of sleep, what with the baby and all." The words were no sooner out of his mouth than Jack realized he'd made a tactical error. Quickly he picked up his cup and drank coffee.

Gina's smile was knowing. "Oh, so you spent the night at Rachel's? Because of the snow, bad driving conditions, and so on, I imagine, eh?"

He gave it up. "All right, so you caught me. Rachel's...a very nice person."

"A nice person. Mmm-hmm." It pleased her to make him squirm just a little. "Every woman's dream, to be thought of as a *nice person* by a man she's interested in."

He leaned back. "What makes you think Rachel's interested in me?"

Gina finished her muffin and wiped her mouth on the flimsy little paper napkin. "Because I have eyes and saw the two of you together." She raised a hand to wave off a protest she was certain he'd raise. "Don't bother denying it. Both of you were as transparent as tissue paper." Elbows on the table, she looked at him. "Let's get back to Alyssa. What's Rachel going to do?"

Jack shrugged. "Take care of her until the father,

whoever he is, returns, I suppose. She's out right now buying all kinds of things—food, clothes, a bed.''

"Because she's a nester, Jack.''

"Well, I'm not, so you can just put away your little matchmaking kit because it's not going to work." He drained his cup and reached into his pocket for his wallet. "Thanks for meeting with me." He glanced out the window. "At least the snow's stopped." There was perhaps three inches accumulated, but the salt trucks had already hit the major streets.

"I hear that Ellis Montgomery's very prejudiced, especially against Native Americans,'' Gina said. "What did he say about the baby?''

Jack scanned the bill and put some money on it. "He's out of town and hasn't seen Alyssa yet. But he's due home tonight and all hell may break lose.''

So Jack and Rachel had driven away from her home last night and gone to the Montgomery house where no one was around, Gina surmised. And Jack had spent the night. Maybe Rachel would be able to do the impossible, to get her brother to settle down. She was certain that Jack needed love more than just about anyone she knew, yet he'd die before he'd admit it. She'd have to keep an eye on things. She'd just met Rachel, but she didn't want Jack to hurt her. Or vice versa.

"Listen, if Ellis gives Rachel a hard time, tell her she can bring Alyssa to our home until she makes other arrangements.''

"That's very nice of you. I'll tell her." He slid out of the booth, leaned down and kissed her gorgeous hair. "See you later.''

Gina watched him drive away through the picture window, the heavy car slip-sliding only a little on the slick pavement. Later on, she'd call Rachel, she decided, rising with just a little difficulty. It never hurt to put in a good word here and there.

"Eat your breakfast." Micky Culver wondered how she could go on day after day on what she ate. Audra was so thin already, and in the last few months she seemed to have lost more weight. "I swear I don't understand how you don't waste away."

"Leave me alone, Micky," Audra said in a huff. She ran a hand through her close-cropped, bleached-blond hair. "I need a cigarette." She looked around at the packed Hip Hop Café, at the faces of the people she lived among but didn't really care to know. "Let's get out of here." Without waiting for Micky, she got up and left.

Outside she lit up and scuffed her boots in the light snow. When she heard Micky behind her, she turned to have it out with him. She couldn't take his demands anymore, his constant hawking her, watching her every move. She couldn't stand *him*. She deserved better. It was over—now she'd tell him. But, as if sensing what she planned to say, it was Micky who spoke up.

"I know."

That was all he said, but the two tiny words nearly toppled Audra like a heavyweight's punch to the belly. She tried to hide her shaking hand and forced a smile. "What are you talking about, baby?" she asked sweetly. "What do you know?"

Micky looked up and down the snowy street, his ponytail swinging in the wind, his hoop earrings swaying. As if convinced no one could overhear, he leaned down close to her face and tugged on the zipper of her torn down vest till her neck was exposed. "Where's your locket, Audra? Haven't seen it since...well, about late August." He smiled a sick smile. "Lose it somewhere?" he asked. "Like a crime scene?"

Audra nearly reeled backward. Her mind raced and her pulse pounded so hard, she thought she'd faint right here in the middle of town. How did he know? How could he know? She put out the cigarette, smashing the butt hard with the toe of her boot, wishing it was Micky she was rubbing out. She had no choice but to deny it, deny everything. Then she'd take him home and, no matter how repulsive the thought was, take Micky to bed. Sex had always smoothed things over before. Yeah, that's what she'd do.

But Micky just pushed away her hand as it reached out for his chest. Then he clutched her arm in his strong fist, his fingers encircling her upper arm and biting hard into it. "Cut the act. I know what you did to that Montgomery girl. I saw how you hit her on the head, how you killed her." His brown eyes blazed, then suddenly cooled. "I followed you to the hills that night. I saw you digging, then swing that shovel when she came up on you."

"But, Micky, it was an accident. She scared me. I—"

"Accident?" He snorted at her defense. "I don't

think so. Not when you followed her down the embankment and hit her on the head with a rock. Trust me, honey, that looked real deliberate—even to me. And I ain't no genius.''

"No, Micky, it wasn't like that." Audra threw frantic glances up and down the street, trying hard not to make it look like a confrontation, not to draw attention from the busybodies opening up their shops or on the other side of the windows in the Hip Hop. All she could think about was getting out of here, where they could be seen. Any moment and the sheriff or his deputies could be walking down the street for a cup of coffee from the café. She had to make Micky go home. Then she'd find a way to get to a phone and call Lexine. Her mother would know what to do.

"Let's go home, Micky, and I'll explain everything. I'm sure you'll understand."

"Oh, I understand, all right." He smiled and let go of her arm, but the smile didn't reach his eyes. He reached out and smoothed her vest, then a lock of hair that was sticking on end. "What I understand is that from now on, you'll be doing exactly what I tell you. When I tell you. Starting right now, when you'll be moving back in with me."

No matter how repulsive the thought of moving back into his filthy trailer, of sharing a bed with him again, she forced her trembling lips into an answering smile. "Sure, Micky. Whatever you say."

"That's right, babe," he said through his teeth, as he proceeded down the street, with her on his arm. "Be nice. 'Cause if you don't, I'll march right over to our Sheriff Rawlings.'' He cocked his head in the direction of the station. ''And you'll find yourself in prison—right next to your mother.''

Sloan Ravencrest motioned Jack into his office through the open doorway while he finished his phone call. Jack sat across from the deputy, wondering if Sloan would know anyone from the reservation who might have been seen with Christina and could possibly be Alyssa's father.

''I'll take care of that, Rafe,'' Sloan spoke into the receiver as he jotted notes on a pad. ''Talk with you later.'' He hung up the phone, made a final note, then leaned back in his swivel chair. ''Good morning, Jack. How are things going?''

''Not too bad,'' Jack answered. ''Have you discovered anything more about Christina's death?''

''Can't say I have, although we should have the autopsy report in another day or so. I finally tracked down every single name on that list, but I can't honestly say I have even one suspect that looks remotely guilty. How'd you do?''

''I questioned a few, but I don't think the baby's father is on that list. We had a surprise last night around midnight at the Montgomery house. Someone dropped a baby girl, about three months old, in a basket on the porch, just like in the movies, with a note asking Rachel to care for the child until her father can come back for her.''

Jack and Rachel had discussed revealing Alyssa's whereabouts until she'd finally given in on letting Jack tell Sloan. She wasn't doing anything illegal, the note giving her permission to care for the child, and Jack felt it was important to keep Sloan apprised, to keep his trust so he'd also share information.

"No kidding? Rachel is sure the baby's Christina's?"

"Absolutely. The age is right, she's got these big blue eyes and the same birthmark, a crescent moon, on the sole of her right foot, that all of the Montgomerys have. But that's where the resemblance to Christina ends." Jack crossed his long legs and raised his gaze to Sloan. "She's got straight black hair and Native American features." He watched the surprise move into Sloan's dark eyes.

"That kind of narrows our playing field." Swiveling his chair, he stared out the single window in the small office, lost in thought for a minute or two.

"You wouldn't happen to know anyone living on the res who'd been seen with Christina, do you?" Jack asked carefully.

Shaking his head, Sloan swung back. "Not offhand, but I'm going to compile a list of all the eligible men and question them."

"Eligible? What if he's married? That might explain the secrecy."

"What kind of shape is the baby in?"

"Well cared for, chubby, happy." He'd awakened to little cooing sounds about six, Rachel awake and giving Alyssa a bottle. By the time he'd showered and gone downstairs, she was rocking the baby in the chair by the fireplace, her face aglow. Jack had stood there for several minutes, struggling with new, unwelcome emotions as he'd watched the two of them.

He wasn't sure what he'd felt. He only knew that the sight of them had been disquieting, disturbing him in a way he couldn't explain.

"I can't imagine any man whose wife would care for a baby for months," Sloan said. "Her husband's baby, but not hers. More likely I'm looking for some guy who's taken care of this baby really well by himself for three months and suddenly, for reasons unknown, leaves her in the middle of the night with Rachel." Sloan shook his head. "I go to the res often. I've got a lot of friends there. News like this spreads quickly. In all this time, I haven't heard a thing about anyone with a baby."

"Would you mind if I go to the reservation and ask around?"

Sloan straightened in his chair, his look skeptical. "You can try, but I doubt you'll get much cooperation. It's kind of a close-knit community. They don't trust outsiders. Nothing personal."

"Then I won't waste my time, not if you're going to ask around and keep me informed."

"I told you I would, and I appreciate you coming in and telling me your news. By the way, what did Ellis Montgomery say about the baby? Indians aren't his favorite folks."

"Don't know," Jack said, rising. "He's been out of town. He's due home this evening. Should be interesting."

In more ways than one, Sloan thought, becoming aware of the timetable, that Jack had to have been at the house at midnight and Ellis not home. Well, why not? Rachel was certainly a lovely woman.

"Better brace yourself," Sloan warned. "It's going to hit the fan."

"You're probably right." Jack stood and turned toward the door, then turned around at Sloan's call.

"One more thing, Jack. Tell Rachel I'll be by to check out that little girl as soon as I get a chance. I'll arrange DNA testing on her and Christina for positive ID."

"Right." With that, Jack left, thinking he'd go to Rachel's to see if she was home from her shopping spree.

Rachel gazed at the baby contentedly sleeping in her basket near the hearth, and her eyes filled with tears. The sadness was for her sister, that she would never know this beautiful child.

What had happened on that rocky hillside that August day when Christina had given birth, then died? Had she been alone? If not, who had been with her? What had gone through her mind in that terrible lonely time?

Rachel wiped at the lone tear, overwhelmed with guilt. She should have paid more attention, should have kept track of Christina, should have returned more frequently. Never mind that her sister hadn't wanted her interference, she should have insisted. Hindsight. It was wonderful, but useless.

The doorbell ringing startled her and she shot a glance at Alyssa, but the baby didn't stir. She'd worn out the poor child, dragging her shopping most of the morning.

Rachel hurried to the door before the visitor hit the

bell again, and opened it. "Jack, I'm so glad to see you." And she was, her emotions close to the surface, her feelings unguarded.

"You're crying," Jack said, walking in and closing out the cold. "What's wrong?"

"I'm just sad that my sister had to miss out on raising her child."

He removed his jacket and took her into his arms, placing a kiss on her sweet-smelling hair. "That's a shame, but at least Alyssa has the next best thing. You."

Rachel slipped her arms around him, inhaling deeply the pine aroma of the outdoors and his own clean masculine scent. Tall and solid, he was like a tower of strength, one she was glad was around right now. She wanted to share her excitement.

"Come look at the things I bought," she said, taking his hand and leading him into the living room to see the boxes and bags spread on the couch, a chair, even the hearth.

"Sort of bought out a store or two, didn't you?"

"I did get carried away a little." She began dragging out little sleep sets and undershirts and socks, sweaters, two dresses and a snowsuit. There were more bottles, cans of formula, blankets, rattles. And finally, a portable crib plus a colorful mobile to hang above it. "What do you think?"

"I think Alyssa's one lucky little girl." He couldn't ignore the excitement in Rachel's eyes, her cheeks flushed, her lips smiling. He kissed her soundly. "You did good, babe." The child looked satisfied and Rachel had even built a fire. She was a born nurturer.

"You really think so? I mean, the poor little thing came to us with the bare essentials. I didn't get things like a high chair or a stroller or a real bed because…well, I'm not sure how long I'll have her."

"Wise move." Jack hoped Alyssa's father wasn't using Rachel for an interim place to park her while he worked things out, one day to return and take her away, but it very much appeared that was the case. "It's going to be hard for you to not get too attached. She'll be returning to her father, you know."

"Yes, yes, I know." But she didn't want to think about that right now, because it would also mean the case would likely be over and there'd no longer be a reason for Jack to stay. Already this morning, he'd been on the phone with his office, checking on his other cases. His other life was calling him back. "So, tell me about your morning."

But before Jack could, they heard a key turn in the door lock and watched as Ellis Montgomery crossed the threshold into the entryway, closing the door behind him.

"Damn cold out there," he said with a shiver before carefully placing his Stetson on the hall table. He glanced into the living room and saw his daughter with that private investigator whose car was parked in the driveway and his whole demeanor soured.

"Hello, Dad," Rachel said, aware that Ellis hadn't noticed the basket. She sidled over, blocking the baby from his view, delaying the inevitable. "How was your trip?"

"Fine." Ellis hung up his coat before entering the

living room and eyeing Jack who greeted him po-
litely.

"Why are you still here? I thought I made it clear
that we don't need anyone other than the local au-
thorities on my daughter's case." Ellis crossed the
room and leaned close to the fire, warming his hands.

"I hired him," Rachel reminded her father, "And
I—"

A baby cried out once, then louder.

Ellis looked as startled as a deer caught in the head-
lights. Jack seemed surprised, since Alyssa hadn't
once cried that he'd heard since she'd arrived last
night, and Rachel pivoted and leaned down to the
basket.

"Shh, darlin', it's all right. Go back to sleep."
With a light touch, she rocked the basket gently, hoping Alyssa would go back to sleep. The baby closed
her eyes and Rachel turned back to face the scowl on
her father's face. "I can explain…" she began.

"I certainly hope so," Ellis said, his tone impatient.

"Her father came here last night, left the basket on
our doorstep, rang the bell and drove away." She
pulled the note from her pocket. "He asked me to
care for her until he returns."

His scowl deepening, Ellis quickly read the note.
"Who the hell expects you to nursemaid their child
for who knows how long? His kid, his responsibility.
Take her back to him."

Rachel sucked in a calming breath, trying not to
feel as though she were fifteen and being called on
the carpet for missing curfew. "I don't know who he

is, so I can't take her back. Besides, I don't want to take her anywhere. She's Christina's baby and belongs with us."

"Christina's baby?" His voice was loud and incredulous. "What makes you think so?"

"Dad, please, lower your voice. You'll frighten her." Rachel glanced at the baby and saw her squirm as if on the verge of fully awakening.

"This is *my* house and I'll shout if I want to." Ellis was growing more impatient and angry by the minute.

"She's got Christina's blue eyes and—"

"Hell, half the people around here have blue eyes."

"Not just exactly like Christina's they don't. More importantly, she's got the birthmark on her foot. Just like her mother had and I have. Max, too. You remember, Dad."

Standing by, deciding it was better if he stayed out of it, Jack was amazed at Rachel's patience with her overbearing, pompous father. He never could have carried it off.

"I don't remember any such thing. Move aside," he commanded his daughter.

Taking in another deep breath, Rachel stepped closer to Jack, felt him take her hand and give it a squeeze, while Ellis leaned down to the basket. She waited for the explosion that was sure to come.

Her father didn't disappoint her. "What the hell is this? This baby's an Indian. She's *not* Christina's child. No, sir. No way." He swung around and glared at Rachel. "Take her out of my house."

"Dad, Sloan's ordering a DNA test that will prove

what I already know to be true. This baby is Christina's.''

"Damned if it is.'' Ellis's face was red with fury. "No daughter of mine would bed down with an Indian.'' He marched back to the vestibule, grabbed his coat and shrugged into it. "I'm going out for a couple of hours. When I get back, she'd better be gone.''

"Then I'll be gone with her,'' Rachel said defiantly.

"Fine with me.'' Ellis placed his Stetson squarely on his head, opened the door and left, slamming it for emphasis.

Rachel tried to compose herself, to push aside her own anger at her bigoted father. "I should have known he'd never change. His precious image means more to him than any of us. Always has.'' She glanced at all the baby things she'd picked out with such loving care earlier today, her mood happy and hopeful then. In ten minutes Ellis had pulled the rug out from under her, leaving her feeling overwhelmed and bereft.

Jack searched for the right words. "Listen, I had coffee with Gina this morning. She knows what Ellis is like and told me you and Alyssa are welcome at their home as long as it takes you to make other plans.''

Rachel blinked at tears threatening to fall over the kindness offered by a woman she's only recently met. "Thank her for me, but we can't impose like that.'' Squaring her shoulders, she walked to gaze out the window, desperately needing a plan of action.

"She meant it, Rachel. Gina wasn't just being polite.'' He moved up close at her back and slipped his arms around her.

''I know she meant it. Gina's awfully sweet. But I've got to find a place of our own.''

''I hate to bring up something else that might be upsetting, but aren't you scheduled to go back to your job in Chicago soon? How are you going to take care of this baby in Montana and maintain your job, too?''

''I've talked with my head designer and arranged for an indefinite leave of absence. I have a good deal of time coming and I don't think they want to lose me permanently.''

Rachel wanted to lean back into his strong arms, to close her eyes and make the world go away. But she couldn't. She had a small baby depending on her now. Suddenly, an idea occurred to her.

Turning, she glanced around the room, as if searching for something. ''Where did I put yesterday's paper?''

Jack spotted it. ''Over on the footstool.''

''Thanks.'' Quickly, Rachel found the section she wanted and hastily paged through it. ''There it is. I went to school with Ruth France. She's the only real estate agent worth anything in Whitehorn. She sells houses but also rents out cabins for summer visitors. However, during the winter months, most of them are vacant.''

Memorizing the number, Rachel headed for the phone, tossing a smile over her shoulder at Jack. ''I'm going to rent the first nice cabin Ruth can find for me. Then I'm going to move Alyssa and me into it.''

Seven

"How does this color strike you?" Jack asked, stepping back from the wall, paintbrush in hand.

Rachel cocked her head, considering, her eyes traveling between the latest streak of paint and comparing it with the other two. "I think the second one's the prettiest. What do you think?"

"I think you'd better make up your mind soon because I'm not going back to the store again if one of these three doesn't suit you," he said, his voice exaggerating patience. "Do you really think Alyssa will be fussy about what shade of pink her room is painted?"

"Yes, she will. The Montgomerys have a real sense of color." She bent to where he was fastening the lid on the rejected can and kissed the top of his head. "You're sweet to offer to paint her room."

Sweet. Yeah, that was exactly how he viewed himself, Jack thought with a frown. "Glad you think so." "Sappy" might fit him better. Since meeting Rachel, or more accurately since Alyssa's arrival, he'd found himself doing all sorts of "homey" things he'd never done before.

When Ellis had stormed out after seeing Alyssa that day, leaving Rachel in need of a place to stay right away, Jack had to help her. The Realtor Rachel knew had immediately set up several appointments to view available rentals. Naturally, he'd gone with her because someone had to drive while Rachel kept watch over the baby, who was in a car seat, and looked over the properties.

She'd finally chosen a two-bedroom cabin off Silver Creek Road. Jack had to admit the little house had a lot of charm, nestled the way it was among the pines with a stream along the back lot line, the water frozen now, of course. There was a great room with a fireplace and bookcases, the carpeting new, the furniture oversize and comfortable. The kitchen was fairly large and surprisingly modern, as were the two baths. The master bedroom had oak furniture, including a big four-poster, but the second bedroom had been empty.

Rachel had gotten permission to decorate it as she saw fit. That was where Jack had come into the picture.

First, he'd helped move them in that very night. After all, Ellis had told her he wanted both of them gone by the time he returned. So Jack had put Rachel's suitcase into the Lincoln's big trunk along with all the things she'd purchased for the baby, and the three of them had driven to the cabin.

Jack had busily arranged to have utilities and phone turned on while Rachel had done some cleaning, not trusting the former tenant's sanitation. That evening, he'd driven some distance to find a pizza joint and they'd eaten the gooey concoction by the fire while sipping the wine he'd also picked up. Studying Rachel in the glow of the firelight, he'd thought she'd never looked more relaxed or happy, even though her whole life had literally been turned upside down for who knew how long.

And she'd never looked more beautiful. After Alyssa cooperated by falling asleep early, they'd crawled into the big feather bed and made love for hours. Her eyes closed, Rachel had snuggled into his arms, but Jack had lain awake for a long while, his emotions in a turmoil.

What was he doing in this domestic scene, the kind he'd always run from? Sure, he loved making love with Rachel, although he knew that thrill would wind down, too. It always had with other women he'd known. He even enjoyed watching her with the baby, amazed at the transformation of a cool professional career woman turning into a picture of cooing and cuddling maternal bliss.

But this wasn't his life, his future. This was a break in routine, an unexpected happening, an interim diversion. He was enjoying it simply because being here with Rachel and the baby was so different from his normal, everyday life. Just to be sure he didn't get too far afield, he'd flown back to L.A. last week and stayed five days, getting caught up on paperwork and other ongoing cases. Much to his surprise, Ronnie Drake, the partner he'd taken in after Gina had quit to get married, had been handling things well and all was under control.

Actually, he'd felt as if he wasn't needed, something new to Jack.

Telling himself that the case in Whitehorn hadn't

been settled to his client's satisfaction, he'd flown back. After all, although Christina's baby had been found, her murderer hadn't been caught. Jack wasn't in the habit of leaving until a case was closed. He was needed in Montana to find a killer.

And to paint Alyssa's room. Setting aside the two rejected paint cans, Jack opened the chosen color and stirred the contents.

Humming to herself, Rachel measured the two windows for curtains, occasionally checking on the baby who was napping in her basket in the great room.

"Isn't she due for a bottle soon?" Jack asked, surprising himself at how quickly he'd become aware of Alyssa's schedule. Domesticity snuck up on a guy when he was busy daydreaming about the woman in question. Next thing he knows, he's reeled in like the fish of the day.

Only that wasn't going to happen to Jack Henderson. He was not marriage material, and certainly not a father figure. He'd made that clear to Rachel and was certain she knew how he felt. Not that she had any intentions along those lines, either, he was sure. She'd had a bad experience and wanted nothing to do with marriage. More than likely, she'd needed a break from her job that, although challenging, had been stressful. So she was taking this time to regroup and relax, let her maternal instincts have free reign. But just until Alyssa's father came to claim her.

Rachel was a realist, not a dreamer. When the time came, she'd hand over the child and go back to Chicago. And Jack would return to his life in L.A. Two adults who'd met through circumstances, enjoyed one another during that time and then went their separate ways with no one getting hurt. Because no one had unrealistic expectations. He would hang on to that thought.

"I'll feed her soon," Rachel answered.

"Anything cooking for us big people?" he asked, pouring paint into the tray, then picking up the roller he'd prepared. He'd begun to look forward to her tasty, imaginative meals.

She came up close and squatted beside him. "Just what would this big person want for lunch today?"

He grinned over his shoulder. "You have to ask?"

"Mmm, I believe you had that after dinner last night and again early this morning. Are you trying to wear me out?" Her voice was soft and teasing.

He straightened and brought her up with him, looking at her face, even more lovely without makeup. Long and hard, he stared, as if trying to see the answers to unasked questions in the blue depths of her eyes. "Why is it that I can't seem to get enough of you?" he asked, sounding truly perplexed. He should have been seeing signs of boredom by now, coming up with reasons to move on. Instead, when he'd checked out of the motel before going to L.A., he'd never checked back in. When he returned, he'd driven straight to the cabin and moved in with Rachel and Alyssa.

Temporarily, of course. Until the case was solved.

Rachel didn't quite know how to answer him. What had started out as a frivolous question had suddenly taken on an intensity that had his green eyes darkening. "I can't answer that except to say that it's the same for me. I should probably add that it scares me to death.''

''Me, too.'' Why was he pursuing this? Jack asked himself. He'd never been one to talk about feelings. Maybe because he'd never felt quite like this before. ''You know, I've never lived with a woman before, even temporarily. I've lived half my life alone, with the exception of other men on the base.''

Rachel knew she had to be cautious here. ''How do you like it so far?''

''I find I don't mind it nearly as much as I thought I would. You know, the clichés about stockings drying on the shower rod, makeup everywhere. You're not like that. You're very neat.''

She smiled. ''Was that a compliment?''

''Yeah, it was.'' He slipped his arms around her, edging her a little closer. ''Were you always like this…when you lived with Richard?''

She supposed he had to have some curiosity about that. ''I guess so. You met my father, but my mother was even more of a stickler for cleanliness and for what she called the proper way to do things. As I mentioned before, none of us kids was permitted to leave our room unless fully clothed, beds made, room straightened.''

''Wow! Not even to go the bathroom?''

''We had to wear robes and slippers even then. She was brought up that way, so that's what we were taught.''

''From what I've heard of Christina, I figure she must have had trouble with all those rules.''

Her hands on his chest, she stroked his soft T-shirt,

feeling the strong muscles beneath. "She did, although she didn't turn really rebellious until after Mom died."

"Were you like that when you were with Richard, then?"

"When I went away to college and lived in a dorm with all girls, everything changed. There was very little privacy. Everyone ran around half-dressed. I fell in step."

But he wanted to hear about the man she'd nearly married, for reasons he couldn't explain even to himself. "Did you love Richard?"

She'd been waiting for him to ask, yet wondered why he would if he had no serious interest in her. "I thought I did, or I wouldn't have agreed to marry him. But, although he touched me, he never touched my heart." *That, only you have done.* Silently she watched him.

"You believed in love back then, apparently. What changed your mind?"

Rachel frowned. "I don't know that I've changed my mind because I don't think I ever said I didn't. I still believe in love, but I think it's difficult to find, often hard to recognize, and nearly impossible to explain." She raised her eyes to his and saw confusion. "Take your sister and her husband. Do you doubt that they're in love?"

"No, I guess not. But marriage is like a house of cards, ready to fall at the drop of a wrong word or a questionable action. Do you really think that many people achieve happily-ever-after these days, and stay married?"

This line of conversation was so odd, coming from Jack, Rachel thought. Up to now, she'd thought he wanted to avoid the topic of marriage. "Perhaps not, but that's no reason to stop believing. Someone once said that what the mind can conceive and believe, it can achieve."

"That's the mind. What about the heart? Doesn't it come into play somewhere?"

"Yes, but I believe love starts in the mind, then moves to the heart. We see someone and visually they're interesting to us, attractive to the eye of the beholder. Then we get to know them—intellectually, socially, morally, still with the mind. Then physically we react to them and that begins to involve the heart. We find we're on the same wavelength, that our morals and goals are the same, that we like many of the same things. And finally one day we wake up and realize that we care more about their welfare than our own. That pretty much defines the process for me, even though I said it's nearly impossible to explain."

He'd brought this up, but now he wanted lighten the mood. "It's different for men. We're guys, we're easy. Touch me and I'm yours. No debate."

She sent him a look of disbelief. "I don't think so. That's physical involvement you're talking about and, sure, that's easy, for men and women. It's the afterward that's difficult."

He didn't want to talk anymore, so he leaned down and took her mouth, tugging her near. But Alyssa chose that moment to let out a wail.

Immediately, Rachel broke free and turned toward the baby. She cried so rarely that she had to see to her. "I think she's hungry. I'll get her lunch." But she paused to glance at his disappointed face. "Can we take up where we left off later?"

"Sure." Jack picked up the roller, trying not to be annoyed at Alyssa's timing.

Jack tied the last bumper guard in place in the crib he'd just put together and stepped back to gaze around the baby's room. The portable crib hadn't suited Rachel, so she'd gone out and bought a full-size one. She'd insisted it be placed at the far end of the room, away from the windows, the mobile of dancing bears hanging above it. She'd gone to her father's house and picked up the rocker that had been her grandmother's, daring Ellis to notice and call her on it. Just as Jack had predicted, they hadn't heard from him.

Buoyed by that small victory, Rachel had learned when her dad would be out of town and enlisted Jack's aid to drive the Lincoln over to pack up the small chest of drawers that had been in her room since she was a girl. It had fit in the trunk nicely. After he'd unloaded it, she'd had him paint it white while she'd gone shopping and picked out some quirky drawer knobs in the shape of animal heads. A changing table had been her final purchase, but not the end of her decorating.

Jack had to admire the freehand drawings she'd painted on two of the walls—a dancing bear, a waltzing hippo, a lazy cat, a running dog, a soft-eyed cow and a chubby pig. As she put the finishing touches on the monkey, he told her so.

"I had no idea you were so talented," he said sincerely. "These are really good."

"It's my profession, you know. Art. Graphics have graduated to the computer these days, but I still love to draw the old-fashioned way now and then." Stepping back, she decided the tail finally looked right and left the room to wash her brushes in the laundry room sink.

Following her, Jack was curious. "Do you ever do sketches of people?"

"Sure." Rachel washed her hands. "In my closet in Dad's house, I've got half a dozen big sketchbooks all filled. I plan on getting some supplies next time I'm in town. I'd love to draw Alyssa." *And you,* she amended. So when they were both gone from her life, she'd at least have that.

The ringing phone interrupted and Jack went into the living room to answer.

Drying her hands, Rachel followed, interested since they didn't get many calls. From hearing Jack's end of the conversation, she realized he was talking with Sloan and wondered if he had any leads for them about Christina. She couldn't help wondering if Jack was getting tired of playing house since there was so little to do on the case. She suspected he'd leave if something didn't develop soon.

"Thanks for the call." Jack hung up, wondering how Rachel was going to take the news. "That was Sloan. He got the autopsy report." He led her over to the couch where they both sat.

"Okay, tell me."

"Christina died from a blow to the head, a heavy

rock or possibly the blunt end of a shovel.'' He saw her flinch, so he hurried on. ''Apparently they can tell that she'd delivered the baby only a short while before her death. They also were able to get DNA samples from Christina. Sloan wants you to take Alyssa to the Whitehorn Memorial Hospital so they can get a sample of her blood. Or you can take her back to the pediatrician's office.'' Rachel had taken Alyssa to be checked out, and happily had found her in good health.

''Anything else?''

''They found some other dried blood spots and hair fragments in the area that aren't from Christina. They're keeping them for a possible type-match when they get a suspect. But it's possible those samples got there some time before Christina's body was left there.''

Rachel was quiet and thoughtful, picturing the scene, wishing she'd never insisted they go up there.

Jack took her hand, wrapped it in both of his. ''Are you okay?''

She let out a ragged sigh. ''Yes, I guess so. Did he mention questioning any men who live on the Laughing Horse Reservation, men who could have fathered Alyssa?''

''He said he's asked around, but no one admits to knowing her well.''

''Yeah, right.'' Truth be known, Rachel wasn't all that anxious to identify Alyssa's father. She had the uneasy feeling that he was either the man who'd killed Christina or knew who did.

Jack stroked a finger along her jawline, wishing like hell he could solve this thing for her.

"You know what I heard in the background when I was talking with Sloan?" he asked, wanting to change the subject to something far more cheerful.

"What?"

"Christmas music. Sloan said the main streets are all decorated, the shops and stores, even the sheriff's office. He said we should drive over and take a look."

Christmas. She'd almost forgotten that Christmas was fast approaching, already the middle of December. Driving around to see the lights seemed like such a family thing to do that she was surprised Jack had suggested it. "You want to go?"

"Yeah, I kind of do. I'm curious how you small-town folk celebrate the holiday."

"Nothing as elaborate as you city slickers, I assure you. I remember every Christmas one of our neighbors, Mr. Shaw, used to drive his daughter, Linda, who was my age, and Christina and me around to see the houses all decorated with lights. Carolers would be walking door to door, singing. Max was too above it all, being older, but Chris and I looked forward to that every year." Unaware that a look of melancholy colored her features, she stared into the fire.

Not her father or even her mother, but a neighbor had been the one to take them. He'd meant to cheer her and had instead dislodged another sad memory. But Jack wasn't one to give up. "Why don't we wait until Alyssa wakes up, then take her for a drive since it gets dark quite early. I'll bet she'd love seeing shiny colored lights."

He was willing to step out of character for her, and she loved him all the more for it. "I'd like that."

Pleased at her response, Jack took it a step further. "Afterward, we could go out to eat. Not at the Hip Hop, but at that other place. What's it called? Oh, yeah, Neela's. Want to?"

The prospect of an evening out finally brought a smile to Rachel's face. "Yes."

As if on cue, they heard the baby fussing in her crib, a sign that she'd been awake awhile.

"I think she heard our plans and she's all for them," Rachel said, rising.

"I'll warm her bottle." Walking into the kitchen, Jack thought that his sister wouldn't recognize him, warming baby bottles and taking rides to see Christmas lights. Truth be known, he didn't recognize himself.

Christmas even came to the women's correctional facility, Lexine Baxter thought sarcastically. The powers-that-be had put up a small three-foot fake tree that they'd decorated with a handful of colored balls and a strand of mangled garland. Not that she cared. The only thing that got Lexine through the days was the thought of getting her revenge. And walking into the visiting center right now was the one person who could help her achieve that revenge.

"Mother, it's nice to see you. You're looking good." Audra Westwood spoke into the telephone that connected her to the imprisoned woman on the other side of the panel that separated them.

More than she could say for Audra, Lexine thought.

The girl looked gaunt and drawn, her heavy makeup looking like black and cherry-red lines striped across her pale face. Was she having trouble? Not that Lexine cared, really, but Audra was the only one who knew about the sapphire mines and Lexine needed her to find the hidden cache that would be her salvation. "What's the matter with you?" she asked, fishing for the tone a caring mother would use.

Audra's eyes instantly welled with tears and she wiped at them with shaking hands.

Weak fool, Lexine thought. What trouble had she gotten into now? Fool or not, though, Lexine depended on her, and only her. Unless… She remembered her other daughter, Emma, contacting her recently about coming to visit. It was certainly convenient of Emma to show up now. Especially if Audra was going to be no good to her.

"It's M-Micky," Audra was saying on a quiet sob. "He knows about—" She stopped suddenly, then took a breath and continued. "He's making me miserable, Mother. He's made me move back in with him and he's bossing me around."

The girl's nasal whine was more than Lexine could take. Couldn't Audra see that she was the one suffering here behind bars?

"I've told you before, Audra," Lexine said in a somewhat harsh tone. "You need to stand up for yourself and take what you want. No one's gonna hand you anything in life. Maybe if you cleaned yourself up, you could find a real man, not a loser like Culver." She dismissed the subject with a wave of her hand. "I didn't summon you here to talk about your problems. Have you found the mine?"

Audra sniffled and tried to steady her voice. "You don't understand. I can't go back there." Despite the effort, her swollen eyes looked downright scared. "He…he's watching me. He knows what happened there."

Lexine had no patience left. "What are you rambling about now?"

Her estranged daughter looked her right in the eye and said in an emotionless voice, "I killed someone there. Christina Montgomery. And Micky knows."

Without reacting to the monotone, not even so much as a blink of an eye, Lexine asked, "How could you have been so stupid to get caught? Tell me what happened."

And like the dutiful daughter, Audra did. She told Lexine the whole sordid tale of being surprised by Christina out in the hills and of hitting her over the head. She told her how the murdered woman had grabbed her locket and how Audra hadn't realized it was missing until days later.

"I—I don't know what to do," she said on a shaky breath. "But I do know I'm not going back up to the hills. I'm not going anywhere near there again. So I won't be looking for your mine anymore." Audra sat taller in her chair and raised her chin. "I'm sorry, but I can't take a chance. Not when Micky can turn me in at any time. You'll have to find someone else to help you." Audra looked pleased with herself, as if she'd been practicing the little speech and was proud that she'd been brave enough to deliver it.

Lexine wasn't exactly a receptive audience. Her eyes narrowed and she leaned closer to the partition, trying hard to rein in her blood pressure, which raced out of control. She hoped her face didn't redden and give away her anger. "Is that so, my daughter?" she said in a sweet voice. "Well, I think you're just upset. Why don't you let me help you with…your little problem with the law. After all, that's something I know a lot about." She smiled at Audra, but her eyes were cold as the wind that ripped down from the Crazies in winter.

Audra, who had been staring her straight in the eye, averted her gaze suddenly. She shrunk back in the chair, looking leery and frightened. She got the message, all right, loud and clear.

"It'll be all right," Lexine crooned. "Mommy will think of something…now that I know your secret."

Rachel sat on a tree stump in the backyard, sketchbook in hand, her eyes on the scene in front of her, then down at her drawing. Jack had left early this morning after convincing Sloan to show him around the reservation, and the baby was down for her morning nap after a bottle. Rachel had some time to herself and had been itching to sketch since picking up some supplies.

The temperature hovered around thirty so she couldn't stay out too long, though she was warmly dressed. It had snowed again last night, just a couple of inches, enough to snarl traffic and leave the landscape with a clean covering. Pine trees of varying heights flanked the frozen stream. A shivery Western meadowlark huddled on a barren limb, eyeing her. Snow blanketed most of the backyard, pristine and white, untouched. It was cold, but the wind had died down altogether. Her busy hand sketched away as in her mind she imagined what all this would look like in the spring.

The Ponderosa pines would be fuller. The dormant grass would once more be bright green. The stream would be flowing over rocks she could see only the tops of from her chilly perch. A soft breeze would warm her cheeks and the little bird would no longer be shivering, would instead be singing.

Montana in full bloom was beautiful, she remembered. Far too few months did the landscape look like that, but it was hardly different than Chicago. The winters there could be beastly with the wind whipping the cold from frozen Lake Michigan and spreading it liberally all over the city. The short walk from her apartment to her office on winter days seemed interminable. She rarely took a cab, choosing to tough it out, but she still didn't like it.

However, moving back here wouldn't be such a drastic change in weather. It would be a culture shock, though, as it had been going in the other direction nine years ago. There she had designer shops available, theater, fine restaurants and amenities galore— and the money to indulge in much of them, all of which she'd gotten quite used to. Back in Whitehorn, she'd be able to buy only the bare essentials at local stores, necessitating a drive to Bozeman for most everything else. There was no theater, no five-star restaurant, no designer clothes.

Money might be a problem. Oh, she had a hefty portfolio, for which she had her father to thank. The family had inherited money even before Ellis founded the bank, and he'd invested on behalf of each his children. After Ellis entered politics, Max had taken over her investments and done very well for her. She got monthly reports on all of it, her dividends reinvested each month. She could change that, have the dividend checks sent to her and use that money for living expenses for a while. But it had been ingrained in Rachel since childhood to never touch her capital and to help it grow by leaving the dividends in.

Using her gum eraser, she changed the shape of the bird, hurrying to finish before the cold little thing flew off or froze to death.

So, if she gave up her job at Kaleidoscope, Rachel thought, she'd cut off a lucrative income, which she'd been using for living expenses. Of course, living expenses would spiral downward here in Whitehorn. She could freelance, of course, but it was questionable how many of her clients would remain with her if she "moved to the boonies," as Pete Ambrose chose to describe her home state. Since he was her boss, she'd merely smiled at his little joke, especially since she'd secretly agreed with him for years.

But did she now? She asked herself, shifting to sit more comfortably on the stump. What really did she have to return to in Chicago? A nice apartment, but here, she could dig into her capital enough to buy a house and have no rent to pay. The furniture and clothes she'd accumulated—all good, solid pieces—

she could have shipped. Friends. Yes, she had a few she'd miss, but not that many.

A working single woman in a metropolitan city tended to spend a lot of time at her job if she wanted to get ahead, which left little time to socialize. Many of her co-workers were married and raising families in the suburbs, people she'd had little in common with. She knew only one other person in her building, Lottie Dorchester, the divorced woman in the next apartment. They looked after one another's plants and collected each other's mail when one or the other was out of town. But they'd never socialized.

Would she miss the job, the work, since there was a good deal of creativity involved? Yes, probably. But then again, she'd have time to spend on a project she'd longed to do for years and never found the time for. An illustrated children's book. In her head, she had many of the details worked out.

And now she had a live model to sketch into her proposed book. Rachel smiled whenever she thought of Alyssa. She was such a happy baby, a good baby. On her tummy, she'd lift her head and look around. Last night, Rachel had spread a pink baby blanket on the carpet in front of the fire and put Alyssa down. She'd bobbed her little head around and even rolled over onto her back, surprising herself. She'd squealed with delight at her own feat. Rachel and Jack had sat watching, smiling at her antics.

Yet today, Rachel felt uneasy. Jack and Sloan were bound to find Alyssa's father one day soon. If he wasn't involved in Christina's death, he'd undoubtedly want his daughter back. If he was and would have to go to prison, he'd need someone to raise her. The part that bothered Rachel was not knowing if any moment someone would snatch Alyssa away. Of course, as her aunt, she'd have some rights, but it wasn't the same as raising her.

Rachel closed her sketchbook, hugged it to her and stared off into a blue, cloudless sky. And what of Jack? She'd never guessed he could be so domestic. The other night, he'd driven them all over town so she could show Alyssa the Christmas lights on shop windows and decorated homes. Jack had been so patient, stopping here and there, uncomplaining.

But she wasn't fooling herself, not really. He'd never once asked to hold Alyssa, and she hadn't pushed the issue. She remembered what he'd said about steering clear of marriage and fatherhood. She respected that even as she realized more each day what a good husband and parent he'd make. However, it wasn't her call and she certainly wouldn't do anything to try to change his mind. Not anything overt, anyhow.

But she could dream, could hope, could pray. She who had never been enough for a father's unconditional love nor a brother's devotion or enough to keep Richard interested could make a silent wish that this time, things would be different.

Suddenly, feeling the cold, Rachel decided she'd sketched long enough for one day. As she got up to go inside, she heard the Lincoln approaching on the other side of the cabin. Her heart did a little extra thump as it always did knowing she'd see Jack again.

Yet she didn't know whether to hope he'd learned the father's identity or not.

Hurrying inside, she checked to see that Alyssa was still asleep before going out front. Her eyes grew wide at what she saw. Jack was standing by the trunk of the Lincoln, which had a big fir tree sticking halfway out.

"What is that?" she asked, stepping off the front porch.

"Our Christmas tree," Jack answered, bending to untie the heavy twine that had anchored the tree. Straightening, he smiled as Rachel walked over. "Can't have Christmas without a tree," he stated emphatically, pleased by the look of pleasure on her face. "What do you think?"

"I think it looks really big." She turned to him. "And we have no decorations or a stand or lights."

"Oh, I wouldn't say that." He pointed toward the back seat.

Rachel opened one door and gasped out loud. "Oh, my!" There had to be a dozen boxes piled inside.

He came to her, cupping his hands and blowing warm air on them. Buying a tree had been an impulse he couldn't ignore, not after the night they'd driven around viewing the lights and he'd seen the almost childish wonder on Rachel's face. He hadn't had many happy holidays himself, but that was because his father had left and his mother hadn't been able to cope. But with Rachel, she had both parents right there, yet had had to rely on a neighbor for a little Christmas joy.

Not this year, not if he had anything to say about

it. It was the least he could do because she'd given him a lot of pleasure.

"It's Alyssa's first Christmas. She has to have a tree."

Eyes suspiciously moist, Rachel nodded. "Did you remember to get a stand?"

"Yes, ma'am." He saw that her cheeks were red. "You look cold. Have you been outside?"

"I was doing some sketching in the back." She glanced from the trunk to the boxes. "Which should we take in first?"

Jack pulled her into a bear hug, then placed his hands on her cool cheeks, framing her face. "Are you happy?"

Rachel blinked and a tear escaped before she could stop it. "Yes, very happy. Thank you." Rising on tiptoe, she pressed her mouth to his and, as always her heart fluttered at the contact.

"Mmm," Jack moaned into her mouth as his lips caressed hers. Even through both heavy jackets, he felt her heart, or was it his? Arms encircling her, he deepened the kiss because it had been some four hours since he'd last kissed her. It shocked him that he kept count.

Finally he let go and smiled into her face. "You deserve more happy moments. They agree with you."

She could think of nothing to say to that so she stepped back and began searching among the boxes for the tree stand.

"Did your family put up a tree every year?" Jack asked Rachel as he stooped by the plug to test a string of lights.

"Oh, sure." Rachel opened boxes of ornaments and laid them out on the coffee table, marveling at the lovely assortment Jack had purchased. "My mother had a decorator tree delivered from Bozeman. It was an artificial one, of course. Real ones were too messy. It was white with little red balls for ornaments and little red bows spaced just so at precise intervals. And it had gold roping looped around. There was a beautiful handmade rug spread around the base of the tree, but we weren't allowed to put gifts there. It would have spoiled the effect."

Jack heard the bitterness beneath her words and felt much as he had years ago when he'd tried to give his sister some good Christmas memories. "We couldn't afford a tree, not with my meager earnings. We barely could afford food and clothes. But we had some old decorations from back when my dad had been around and still working. So Gina used to take the somewhat ratty red roping and wind it around the lampshades. And she'd hold the chair while I stood on it and hung the ornaments from string stuck to the ceiling with tape."

Sitting beside the canvas bouncy chair she'd picked up for Alyssa, which the little girl loved, Rachel felt her heart break for the two young children who had such sad holidays. "What about your mother? Didn't she take part?"

He shrugged as he stood and began stringing lights on the tree, now ensconced in its stand, the top reaching almost to the ceiling of the living room. "She tried, I guess. My memories of her during my early teens are as if I'm looking through smoke. She was there, only she wasn't. She used to sit and stare out the window a lot with this vacant look on her face, drinking coffee and smoking cigarettes. I think it was her way of escaping the terrible reality she was suddenly facing. And, of course, she blamed our father for leaving.''

''That must have been awful for you and Gina.'' At least, the Montgomery house had been full of people, socially prominent people her mother had invited from her clubs and political men and their wives Dad had invited. Of course, Rachel hadn't really known any of them, but there'd been noise and laughter and lots of food.

''It wasn't so bad because Gina and I were together. She was great. Even when she was really young, six or seven, she memorized all the words to the Christmas songs and we'd turn on the radio and sing along. She'd draw Mom and me little notes, first crayon pictures, later with poems she'd make up. I still have some of them in an old trunk.'' He frowned as he came around from behind the tree, needing another string of lights. ''You know, I've never told anyone that before.''

Rachel put a small rattle into Alyssa's hand, fastening her tiny fingers around it before rising. Jack was reaching for the last string of lights when she went to him and hugged him from behind. ''You're very special, you know that?''

He turned in her arms and gave her an embarrassed smile. ''I wouldn't go that far.'' He gathered her close. "It's sort of ironic, I think, that neither of us had very many happy Christmases yet in very different ways. I used to wish for pots of money so I could get Mom back to where she used to be, and so I could make Gina happy. Your family had money yet you, and I'll bet Christina, too, weren't happy. Goes to show you, money's not the answer."

No, loving someone, being part of a real family, is, Rachel wanted to say. Instead, she kissed him ever so gently.

It was after eleven by the time the tree was completely trimmed, dinner was eaten and Alyssa was asleep in her crib. The fire was dying in the hearth but that was okay. Tonight, they sat on the couch staring at the tree, half its lights blinking pleasantly.

"That's such a lovely angel," Rachel said. "You really outdid yourself." Snuggled in his arms she reached to kiss him. "Thank you for making this the best Christmas I've ever had."

"It's the best for me, too." Living alone in his Los Angeles high-rise, he'd never bothered buying decorations. Often as not, on Christmas Day, he'd gone into the office to catch up on paperwork, knowing the phones wouldn't bother him, turning down invitations that came his way. If the loneliness really got to him, he'd call Gina, who was often celebrating at a friend's house, and talk awhile until it passed.

Rachel yawned and stretched. "It's this country air. Makes me sleepy." She had a thought and decided to act on it. "You know one of the reasons I settled on this house instead of the others is that big claw-footed tub in the bathroom. I think I'll go in and take a long hot bubble bath.'' Turning, she sent him a challenging look. ''Want to join me?''

Jack's eyebrows raised. ''A bubble bath? They'll take away my macho man badge.''

Laughing, Rachel got up. ''I won't tell a soul.''

''Thanks, but I think I'll pass and turn in. Take your time.''

Later, relaxing in the tub amidst fragrant bubbles, Rachel gazed at the floor-length pale pink satin gown hanging on the back of the bathroom door and smiled. Packing in Chicago, she'd impulsively thrown it in her bag at the last minute, and was now glad she had.

She'd promised herself she wouldn't try to persuade Jack to remain with her. But she'd make darn sure he took away some memories that would make him miss her like hell.

Eight

A storm was brewing outside, the heavy restless clouds having drifted in stealthily all afternoon and early evening. They'd started dumping their load of snow on Whitehorn an hour ago and now, as Rachel leaned back in the tub, she heard the wind begin to moan outside the old cabin. A real test of how well the rental was insulated, Rachel thought, hoping her friend, Ruth France, had steered her right when she'd said the place was snug as a bug.

Lazily, she picked up the fragrant, soapy bath sponge and stroked it over her shoulders. She could feel the hot water doing its thing, her muscles relaxing and the tension leaving her. In Chicago, especially in winter, she'd soaked in her tub nearly every night, considering her bath a great stress reliever. She'd pinned up her hair and now lay back, letting her mind drift.

The old timbers creaked and groaned, but the curtains over the small bathroom window didn't move, so apparently the wind wasn't getting in. Rachel hoped the unexpected sounds wouldn't wake Alyssa. She couldn't hear anything through the thick walls and door, but she knew Jack would look in on the baby if she started fussing.

Some minutes later, the water had cooled and rather than add more hot, Rachel stepped out, anxious for the next act to begin. If she stayed too long, Jack would be asleep and though it might be fun to waken him, she wanted him alert and eager. Drying off with a thick towel, she smiled in anticipation.

The scented lotion was next, and she applied it liberally all over her body. The winter winds drained all the moisture from her skin, so this was a nightly ritual, too. Next she brushed her teeth, then put moisturizer on her face, smoothing it on languidly. Finally, she slipped on the gown and watched the soft material fall all the way to her ankles. It was sleeveless, the neckline forming a vee with lace folds criss-crossing over her breasts. Lastly she brushed her hair until it fell in shiny waves to her shoulders.

Ready, she told herself as she slipped her feet into pink slippers and took in a nervous breath. She wouldn't put on her robe for it would definitely spoil the effect. She knew that in the short time they'd been together, Jack had never fallen asleep early, often reading a book in bed until she joined him.

Moving quietly, she opened the connecting door into the master bedroom and stopped in her tracks, stunned.

The room was aglow with a dozen candles of varying sizes and lengths—on the dresser, the two nightstands, a small table by the window—flickering their soft light and filling the room with their seductive scent. The big four-poster had been turned down, the spread laid carefully on the cedar chest at the foot.

The pillows were fluffed and the feather bed in its pale yellow duvet was turned back invitingly. Soft music played from the small radio on the table. On one nightstand stood a bottle of wine and two glasses.

And standing alongside the bed was Jack, still fully dressed except for shoes, holding a sprig of violets in one hand.

"Oh, wow," Rachel whispered, overwhelmed. "You've been busy."

Slowly Jack walked to her. "I remember how much you like candles and romance." He held out the tiny bouquet. "I wanted to get you a rose, but I couldn't find a store that had any in December. I hope you like violets."

"What I like is you," she said, taking one step to close the gap between them. "Thank you for all this."

"Remember, you can't tell anyone. I've got this macho, hard-boiled, ex-detective image to protect." His lips twitched as he smiled down at her.

"Your secret's safe with me." She smiled into his eyes, those gorgeous gold-flecked green eyes. "Looks like a seduction in the making. And here I was going to come out and ravish you."

"We can have a mutual ravishing." He led her over to the wine, poured, then handed her a glass before picking up his own. "To happy days," he said, clinking his glass to hers.

Rachel sipped, enjoying the cool, tart wine as it slid down her throat. She inhaled the sweet fragrance of the violets. "I think I like all this," she confessed.

"I don't believe I've ever been spoiled like this before. Or romanced."

He'd thought as much, had seen the candles in the window of a shop and decided to surprise her. He gazed at her lovely face, thinking she was a woman made for romance. "There's more." He eased her into his arms, his eyes caressing her face. "You're very beautiful, Rachel. I find myself wondering why no man has made you his all these years after Richard."

"I never met a man I wanted enough to become his," she said. *Until now. Until you.*

Carefully, Jack took their wineglasses and set them down, then put her violets next to the bottle. Moving close, he kissed her, letting his mouth tease hers as he eased her onto the big bed, then followed her down. He let his fingers rediscover the softness of her cheeks, tracing the area around her eyes, smoothing away the sadness that lingered there. He followed that journey with his lips, placing soft feather kisses. The wind outside whipped against the windows but he only heard Rachel sigh his name as her arms reached up to welcome him.

They'd both found great satisfaction in their previous bouts of wild lovemaking, but now Jack wanted to show her there was far more than frantic desire. He wanted to show her that there could be a healing pleasure that would satisfy the body and restore the soul. And he hoped it would work on both of them.

He understood how vulnerable she'd been feeling for weeks ever since returning to Montana, her father's open hostility, her brother's indifference, her sister's brutal murder all taking a toll on her nerves and emotions.

So he took her hands and coaxed them to rid him of his clothes, subtly telling her that he would allow himself to be exposed and vulnerable to her. He lay back as she undressed him, her fingers at first hesitant at his belt buckle, then more bold, wordlessly communicating her pleasure at his allowing her to explore him at her leisure.

Jack felt his skin quiver as she slowly unbuttoned his shirt and tossed it onto his jeans already on the floor. Slowly she ran her hands over his chest, burrowing into the hair there, then along his rib cage. Her fingers trailed to his thighs next, her nails scraping along sensitive flesh, and he moaned out loud as his body reacted. He saw a small smile of feminine satisfaction on her face as she skimmed off his briefs and threw them aside.

Her eyes locked with his as she went up on her knees on the bed and seductively ran her hands along her sides, slip-sliding on the soft shimmering satin. She reached out and pulled him up to her so they were inches apart, both kneeling, their breathing ragged and shallow with anticipation.

His gaze still on hers, Jack's fingers found the hem of her gown and caressed the silky material. Slowly he pulled it upward, then quickly tugged it over her head. His eyes drank in her beauty, his heart hammering inside his chest. He stroked the satin gown along and around and between her aroused breasts, then flung it away.

Rachel's face was flushed, but her eyes on his remained steady. Her hands moved to bracket his waist as she lazily brushed her breasts against his chest, back and forth, slowly, maddeningly. Unable to remain passive any longer, Jack crushed his mouth to hers. The kiss went on and on until finally, knees trembling, they tumbled onto the bed, rolling and sighing in the tangled covers. He tasted her hunger, felt her go limp with pleasure, heard the soft murmurings meant only for his ears.

This was what he'd been wanting, Jack realized, this deep awareness of each other, not just that wild race to completion, and it stunned him to admit it. As good as that was, this was another way of making love, a more powerful way and an exciting change. He hadn't craved this sharing of more than just his body with anyone else, but he knew he wanted this with Rachel.

She was moving now beneath him, her hands reaching for him, anxious but not yet desperate. Staying in control, he evaded her clever fingers as his tongue moved almost lazily over first one breast, then the other. He heard her suck in a sharp breath, then arch toward his mouth.

"Are you trying to drive me mad?" Rachel asked, her voice breathless with frustration.

"Yes, that's exactly what I plan to do." His mouth trailed hot fire along her shimmering flesh. He felt her shift restlessly, then cry out as his fingers moved inside her.

She rose to meet him, trying to capture the release he held just a breath away, but he moved out of reach, leaving her needy. Edgy with passion, she felt him trail kisses down her arching body. Then his mouth settled on her as her hands curled around fistfuls of sheet.

The first heady climax surprised her with its intensity, leaving her weak and limp. Ragged breaths puffed from her as she finally looked up to see Jack watching her. Then, so swiftly she felt dazed, he shifted and entered her, dragging her back into the eye of the storm.

Rachel had no time to think, to recover, could only cling to him, her hands skimming restively over his slick back. In seconds, she was racing desperately with him, seeking more and still more, embracing this unexpected bounty she'd been longing for.

Finally, a shimmering wave of pleasure slammed into her, and she was no longer aware of the wintry night or the whistling wind or much of anything else. There was only this candlelit room and Jack and the marvelous sensations she was sharing with him.

And when it was over, Jack held her close, cradling her. He hadn't been able to catch the killer who'd murdered her sister yet. But he'd been able to empty her mind of her worries, her fears, if only for a little while.

Replete, Rachel snuggled into him. Here, like this, lethargic yet glowing from his loving, she felt safe.

Only with Jack. Here she could close her eyes and rest, and no one would harm her.

Drifting into a dream, Rachel sighed. "I love you," she whispered.

In the shadowy glow of the candles, Jack's eyes snapped open. Rachel's breathing was already even, and he knew she likely wasn't aware she'd spoken out loud. But he'd heard and the words left him shaken.

Don't love me, Rachel, he silently told her. *I don't believe in love, not even with you. I'll only hurt you.*

A sound woke him. Always one to awaken quickly, Jack sat up and cocked his head to listen. There it was again, and it was a baby crying. More on target, Alyssa.

He saw that Rachel hadn't heard, fast asleep on her side facing away, so he pulled on his pants and quietly left the room.

The Mickey Mouse night-light on her dresser cast the room in a soft glow. She was wearing her yellow blanket sleeper, zipped up to her neck so she wouldn't be cold. Yet as he walked over to her crib, there were little tears on her chubby cheeks.

"What's the matter, punkin?" Somewhat awkwardly, trying to remember how Rachel did it, he picked her up and brought her close to his chest. "Can't sleep?"

Immediately, she flashed him a smile.

Jack couldn't help it. He smiled back.

He hadn't checked the clock, but it was very dark

outside through her window and snow was still coming down. Gently, he wiped away the tears from her cheeks with his thumb and tried to figure out why she was awake in the middle of the night.

She no longer needed a night feeding so her last bottle had been around 10:00 p.m. Maybe she… whoops! Wet. She was probably really wet, or worse.

Gingerly carrying her over to the changing table, he, who had never changed a baby in his life, decided he could do this. He laid her down and unzipped the blanket sleeper. Rachel had switched her to disposable diapers rather than the cloth ones she'd arrived with. He pulled the side tabs open the way he'd seen Rachel do, first one side, then the other. Sure enough, she was soaking wet.

Relieved that there was no further mess to clean up, he whipped off the old diaper and dropped it into the container alongside the changing table. He found a new diaper on the shelf below, keeping a hand on the kicking baby as he searched. Finally, he opened the diaper, slipped it under her, and fastened it in place. Triumphantly, he looked at her face and saw another smile.

"That feels better, doesn't it? I'll bet you thought I couldn't do that, didn't you? Well, I fooled you." On impulse, he leaned down and nuzzled her face, then remembered his day's growth of scratchy beard and jerked back. "I didn't hurt you, did I, punkin?"

Silently, Alyssa watched him with her big blue eyes.

"Guess not." Working quickly now, more confident, he put her sleeper back together before picking her up. He couldn't help noticing how much more steadily she held her head now that she was nearly four months old. "You're getting so big," he told her.

The problem now was that she didn't look sleepy at all. "Listen, kid, it's sleepy-bye time." He laid her down on her back in her crib, but no sooner had he let go than she rolled over and lifted her head, looking at him, her lower lip trembling.

Hands on hips, he stared at her. "Look, you're dry, not hungry, and it's nighttime. You need to put your head down and go to sleep, all right?"

Good thing no one was here listening to him trying to reason with a baby, Jack thought sheepishly. That was when he spotted her pacifier in the corner of her bed. He stuck it in her mouth and immediately she began to suck away.

But her head was still raised and her eyes still on him.

"What else do you want, hmm? Listen, you'll be fine. Get some rest and I'll see you in the morning." He started toward the door and had gone only two steps when he heard her cry out. Turning around, he saw the pacifier had dropped to the sheet and Alyssa's little face was so sad, her lower lip quivering pitifully.

That got to him.

"Oh, all right," Jack said, giving in, "you win. But only for a little while." He picked her up, stuck the pacifier in her mouth and sat in the rocker.

Arranging her comfortably in the crook of his arm,

he rocked gently, watching her watching him. "You're getting spoiled, you know that? You think you can stick out that lower lip, flash those big blue eyes and men are going to fall at your feet to do your bidding, eh?" He smiled, then laughed out loud when she smiled around the pacifier. "You're going to be a heartbreaker, all right."

Jack settled back, slowly rocking and humming softly, unaware of the tender picture he and Alyssa made.

But Rachel, standing just outside the bedroom doorway, saw it, saw the two people who owned her heart together, the big man and the tiny baby, and her eyes grew moist. Hadn't she known underneath all the macho talk and protests that Jack was an old softie?

Instinctively knowing he wouldn't want to be caught talking and humming to a baby, she backed away and returned to bed, her emotions churning.

Jack sat across from Sloan, who was seated at his desk in the sheriff's office, and knew his frustration probably showed. "I can't believe that not a single person would talk to me, *really* talk to me, on the res. Someone there has to know something. The father of Christina's baby is there, I just know it. But who the hell is he?"

Sloan understood Jack's disappointment and his impatience about solving Christina's murder. Earlier, Jack had told him he'd always "gotten his man." Yet here, everywhere he turned he ran into another dead end.

"I'd apologize if I hadn't warned you they wouldn't open up."

"But I was with you and I could tell they respect you. And still, I could have been talking to that wall over there. They looked right through me and said they knew nothing about a baby who'd been raised by a Native American father for the past three months, not now, not ever."

"Jack, you were with the L.A.P.D. for years and then investigating on your own for more years. You know as well as I that some cases take a long time, years even to get that break needed to solve them."

"Yeah, well, I can usually get someone to open up. I've been here nearly a month, on and off. Not even a slim lead."

"Maybe they were telling the truth," Sloan suggested, "and they really don't know anything."

"Come on. You saw Alyssa. You know she's got Native American blood. They did a DNA workup on her. She's a match with Christina. Therefore, Christina and this Native American mystery man are her parents."

"Yeah, but maybe the guy doesn't live on the res. You have to realize that Native Americans, both male and female, have intermarried in Montana for generations. More recently than in the early years when Indians were shunned by the Whites." He smiled, his handsome face mischievous. "That happened after you-all realized Indians weren't some sort of weird species.''

"Hey, man, don't tie me in with those bigots. I'm from California. We have so many intermarrying nationalities there I doubt there's a purebred in the whole state. And frankly, I think the country's a better place for it. But you and I will never convince the Ellis Montgomerys of the world.''

Sloan nodded in agreement. ''I know you're right and I wasn't lumping you in with Ellis, I assure you. I'm merely pointing out that this guy could be anywhere. He could even have been someone passing through town and is long gone. I wouldn't say this to Rachel, but Christina had hordes of men friends and she wasn't fussy who or what they were. For years I watched her methodically ruin her life and I wondered why.''

Jack crossed his long legs. ''After getting to know Rachel, I think I could make a decent guess. Their mother was an uptight society wanna-be, and Ellis was an absentee father. Max went his own way, and Rachel just wanted to get out. That left Christina, young and with no support, to cope as best she could. Turns out she couldn't cope well at all.''

Jack felt he hadn't revealed any confidences or secrets since most everyone in town knew the Montgomery background and history.

''You're probably right and it's a shame. I suppose Rachel's beating herself up over leaving Christina, now that she's dead. She's the kind who cares too much.''

"Yes, she is and probably always will. I try to tell her that she was young when she left and had to look out for Number One or she'd have been dragged down by that dysfunctional family, too, but naturally, she doesn't buy it. Hell, most of us come from a dysfunctional family. All we can do is the best we can do."

"Amen to that. And speaking of beating yourself up, you shouldn't feel like you've failed in this case. The baby's found and with her aunt who undoubtedly loves her. That's the most important thing. As far as Christina's murderer goes, one day someone will say something someone else will overhear, or someone's conscience will get too heavy and they'll talk to us. Murder is damn difficult to put on the back burner forever, unless the killer is a sociopath."

"That's what I'm afraid of."

"Don't be. Get on with your life. You've done all you can here. If you need to go back to L.A., be assured that I'll call you the minute something breaks."

"Yeah, right." There it was, permission to leave. Wasn't that what he'd been after when he'd come to see Sloan? That way, he could in all honesty tell Rachel that there was nothing further he could do on her case at the moment, that Christina's murder investigation had been placed in the Open and Pending file by the sheriff's department. If he stayed all he'd be doing would be spinning his wheels.

Yet he sat there, silent, thoughtful.

Tossing down the pen he'd been rolling between

his fingers, Sloan leaned forward, his eyes narrowing as he studied Jack. "What is it, Jack?" he asked quietly. "Something bothering you besides this case?"

Jack scraped a hand over his face, then shook his head. "No, don't mind me. One of those days, you know." He gave Sloan a halfhearted smile before rising.

"So, are you going back to L.A.?" Sloan asked.

"Soon, my friend. Real soon." With a wave, Jack headed out the door.

Outside, back in the Lincoln, he found himself frowning. He hated feeling as he did, wanting to stay, needing to go. Yet every minute he remained, he was getting in deeper and deeper.

Hands on the steering wheel, he bowed his head. Rachel had said she loved him. Thirty-five years he'd lived and no woman had ever said those words to him, outside of Gina and probably his mother, years ago when he'd been a boy. Didn't everyone want to be loved? Novels, books, poetry, songs—they all said that love was the answer. So what, then, was his problem?

Here in the silent privacy of his car, he could admit to his problem. He was scared. Scared he'd wind up next year, the year after or the one after that, becoming bored, easily irritated, restless. And he'd move on, as his father before him had done. The Henderson men weren't big on commitment, on follow-through. Rachel deserved better.

He sighed heavily, trying to be honest with himself. He'd been so sure no woman could ever keep him interested for long. Little did Rachel know that she held the record on that score, a record he wasn't necessarily proud of. There was a lack in him, some missing gene or chromosome. She'd come the closest to domesticating him, to getting him to actually enjoy family things, but who knew how long that would last?

And he didn't want to hurt her.

Love had to be life's greatest mystery. He'd never spoken those three little words out loud, always figuring with Gina, who was probably the only person he'd ever truly loved, that his actions spoke his feelings louder than anything he could say. Gina knew he cared, had always known.

But Rachel was another story.

She'd had a lonely childhood and hadn't fared much better since. She deserved some stand-up guy who'd want the whole nine yards—marriage, the house and lots of children, the forever scene. He would even admit that several times over the past few weeks, he'd been happy spending time around the cabin, painting Alyssa's room, drying dishes while Rachel washed, sitting by the fire with her and simply talking. But he knew that wouldn't last, not with him.

Then there was Alyssa. That baby was adorable. Who wouldn't be taken with her? She wasn't fussy, rarely cried, and when he'd held her the other night and rocked her, Jack had felt overwhelmingly protective. Watching Rachel with Alyssa, he couldn't help thinking she should have a whole passel of kids. He just wasn't the man who'd give them to her.

Jack started the car and left the parking lot adjacent to the sheriff's office. She'd find Mr. Right one day, he told himself. She was young, only twenty-seven. Some lucky guy would come along and—

He felt his stomach clench at the thought of some other man touching that satin skin, hearing that funny little catch in her throat when she was nervous, seeing her eyes grow dark and luminous when he made love to her. Unbidden, his right hand formed a fist and he wanted to hit something hard. How many times would similar scenarios play on the screen of his mind after he left her?

His punishment, Jack thought, gritting his teeth. Because already, he would hurt her by leaving, by having stayed too long. She wouldn't love easily, wouldn't say it unless she meant it. So now his leaving would tear her apart and add to her sadness.

It couldn't be helped, he decided. Better now than later when she cared even more. At least she'd have Alyssa to fill her hours. Until she, too, would be taken away by her father returning.

Damn!

Cruising down Main Street, he spotted a shop. One more day till Christmas, he realized. He'd be the dirtiest of dogs if he left on Christmas Eve. Pulling the Lincoln to the curb, he decided he'd find gifts for Rachel and Alyssa. Something to remember him by.

Getting out of the car, Jack noticed that his vision was blurred, something that rarely happened to him. Wiping at his eyes, he went inside.

* * *

Alyssa was laughing as Rachel played peekaboo with her. With her face so close to the baby's, Alyssa reached out and grabbed her aunt's hands, as if to pull them down. Rachel played along and Alyssa laughed again.

Hearing a car approaching, Rachel got up to look out the window. She saw Jack park and go around to the trunk, hauling out package after package. Her heart light, she flew to the door.

"It looks like you've been to see Santa," she said as he stepped onto the porch.

"Yeah, the old guy's feeling generous this year." He bent to kiss her, then strode inside with his bundles, dumping them on the couch. *You can do it,* he told himself. *You can give these two a good Christmas before you go.*

"Hi, punkin," he called out to Alyssa who was now on her tummy on a blanket on the floor, her little head raised, her big blue eyes watching him, a grin on her face. "Hey, I think she recognizes me."

"Of course she does." Rachel took his jacket and hung it up.

Jack paused, gazing at the pile of packages under the tree. "Looks like Santa's already been here."

"Santa as played by Gina and Trent. They stopped by to see the baby and brought us all presents. They were sorry to miss you, but Gina had a doctor's appointment in town so they had to leave."

Jack frowned. "A doctor's appointment?"

"Just her regularly scheduled checkup. Won't be long now, and I think she's getting anxious."

Jack reached into the sacks and began pulling out brightly wrapped packages, then placing them under the tree. He'd had everything wrapped at the store; it had been easier that way. When he finished, he turned to Rachel. "So, do you want to eat dinner first, then open packages? Or are you going to make me wait until morning?" He could smell something wonderful cooking.

"At our house, we always opened our gifts Christmas Eve," she said, going into the kitchen to check the oven. "I made Cornish hens with wild rice stuffing. Dinner should be ready in half an hour."

"Just time enough for us to have a glass of wine," Jack said, reaching into the cupboard.

"Did you learn anything new from Sloan?" She'd been anxious all afternoon knowing where he'd gone, yet she couldn't have said why. Nerves, she supposed.

"Nothing new. Absolutely nothing." He poured wine, not looking at her. "The case is at a standstill."

"I see." Rachel straightened a fork and rearranged a plate on the already perfectly set table, needing something for her hands to do.

He brought the wine to her, held out the glass. "Lots of cases run into snags, Rachel. Then suddenly, someone talks, or a person remembers something and calls. Happens all the time. This doesn't mean we'll never find Christina's killer."

"I know. It's just so…so disappointing."

"Like you, I would have liked to wrap it all up in short order, get the killer behind bars. But these investigations don't work like cases on TV where everything comes together in sixty minutes.''

Eyes downcast, she nodded. *He was leaving. This was the goodbye speech. Have dinner, open gifts, kiss goodbye.* Her heart aching, she tightened her grip on the wineglass, determined that he wouldn't see her hand tremble.

With all his heart, Jack wished he could find the words that would remove that stricken look from her face. She'd guessed that he'd be leaving soon and already she was hurting. She'd hurt more if they dragged this out, if he stayed much longer.

Cupping her chin, he forced her to look at him. When she finally met his eyes, he saw that she'd found the strength somehow to pull herself together. ''Merry Christmas,'' he said softly.

''Merry Christmas,'' Rachel whispered.

Nine

He was packing. It wouldn't take long, Rachel thought, for he'd only brought one suitcase. She could hear him in the bedroom they'd shared for nearly three weeks now as she sat on the couch giving Alyssa a bottle.

Perhaps she should be grateful that Jack had stayed on for nearly the whole week after Christmas. Not much going on with his agency during the holidays, he'd told her after he'd called L.A., nothing pressing that he had to rush back to. In a way, Rachel wished he hadn't stayed. Each day with him, she fell more in love. Each day for her meant it would be all that much more difficult to say goodbye.

Finally, just before the new year, he'd announced this morning that he needed to get back. He'd quickly added that he'd made arrangements with Sloan to call him should anything new develop on Christina's case, and he'd fly back.

Actually, Rachel preferred a clean break. At least with Richard she'd come home to find him packing, the abrupt decision he'd made to leave knocking her for a loop. But she hadn't had days to sit around knowing it was going to take place, but not aware of when. Even though there was no comparison on how she'd felt about Richard as to how she felt about Jack.

Rachel set the bottle down and raised Alyssa to her shoulder to burp her. She hadn't really known what it was like to be in love until Jack. Everyone said it was better to have loved and lost than not to have loved at all. She wasn't so sure about that. Someone who hadn't been through it had probably made that up. Perhaps if asked years from now, she'd agree. But not today.

She could beat herself up over this, for falling in love with him in the first place—since she was so good at shouldering the blame for things that were beyond her control—except she now realized that there was no way a person could prevent love from happening. She'd warned herself not to care too much, not to get involved, not to lead with her chin. But her feelings, those fragile feelings Jack had brought to life, hadn't listened. Without her permission, even without her knowledge at first, she'd fallen head over heels.

She was trying not to be angry as well as hurt, although anger was easier to deal with. She couldn't blame him since he'd told her exactly how things were with him almost from Day One. And she'd believed him, believed that he wasn't just waiting for the right woman to cross his path, but instead he was someone who had decided as far back as his teens that marriage and commitment weren't for him. She had no rival, no woman in L.A. waiting in the wings to embrace him when he returned.

How the hell could you fight a mind-set?

Richard had left selfishly to pursue his own dream, never mind that he'd destroyed hers. Jack was leaving because to stay would compromise who and what he was, or so he said. He was leaving to prevent both of them from even deeper pain, so he'd explained last night after their most poignant lovemaking session yet.

She'd worn only the lovely gold heart-shaped locket on a chain that he'd given her for Christmas. Over and over again, he'd reached for her, and she'd gone into his arms gladly, willingly, knowing that night would be their last together. When he'd finally fallen asleep, she'd gone into the bathroom, closed the door and let the sobs that had been building all week have free rein. She'd cried so hard and so long that she'd lost her dinner. She hadn't returned to the bed they shared until she'd composed herself, until she'd splashed cold water on her face and eyes, until the episode was over.

There'd be more, Rachel knew.

But not in front of him. This morning, she was calm, clear-eyed, pleasant. She'd even joked with him at breakfast. Her mother would have been proud for she'd acted like a true lady, hiding her feelings, avoiding a public display. Rachel with the stiff upper lip and the backbone ramrod-straight, giving no hint of her broken heart. It was a role she hated.

Jack came out of the bedroom carrying his bag, walked over and set it down by the door. In his hand dangled the gold-and-onyx keychain with his engraved initials that she'd given him for Christmas. What with caring for Alyssa, she hadn't had much time to shop, but he'd seemed pleased with her small gift.

He'd outdone himself, getting Alyssa a lovely dress, a big teddy bear and her first pair of shoes, which she wouldn't need for some time yet. Rachel had fared as well with a hand-embroidered sweater and a pure white nightgown with matching robe and slippers. For a man unused to buying for women and babies, he'd even gotten the sizes right.

It had been a lovely Christmas Eve, the best. She'd have lots of time to relive it, Rachel thought as she checked Alyssa and saw she'd fallen asleep. Rising, she carried the baby to her crib and put her down for a nap. When she returned, Jack was standing by the door wearing his jacket, looking uncomfortable.

She would not make this more difficult for him.

"I envy you returning to all that sunshine while we can expect months more of snow," she said with a smile she had some difficulty forming.

Jack drank in the sight of her for the last time. She was wearing a bulky black sweater that came down low on her thighs over black leggings, her feet in pink slippers. He remembered how her hair smelled, how satiny her skin felt, and knew he'd have to live on his memories from now on. She looked small and very pale, so tense that he was certain one wrong word and she'd splinter.

"Yeah, that's one good thing about living in L.A. We may have smog, but it's warm smog, even in winter." He stayed where he was, jiggling his keys, wanting to touch her, to take her into his arms one last time. But he was uncertain how she'd react. "Maybe you could drop me a line now and then. I left my card on the table."

"Maybe." Why would she torture herself like that?

"We always knew we'd face this one day, right?"

"Yes. I hope you find what you want, Jack." Feeling exposed and vulnerable, she crossed her arms over her chest.

"I'm not sure what I want. Do you know what you want?"

"Yes, I think I finally do. I want a home and a family, and I won't settle for less."

Jack shook his head sadly. "I told you from the start, Rachel, that I'm not cut out for marriage."

Sometimes a tautly strung wire breaks unexpectedly. "Oh, bull!" Rachel said, anger mingled with hurt in her voice. "Don't give me that, Jack. I've heard it before. Who *is* cut out for marriage? Certainly I've seen few shining examples, but I've got the guts to pursue that dream anyway."

"You know my father left and—"

"Why can't you be honest, at least? Say you wanted a good time, a few laughs, a little bedtime pleasure, then back to your life in L.A. But quit blaming your father for everything. You're your own man, not someone's robot programmed to follow in his footsteps. If—if I'm not enough for you, be man enough to say so." Her voice was low, level, but trembling.

"It's not that—"

"Please." She'd had enough. If they sparred much longer, Rachel knew she'd break down completely. "Just go." Turning, she faced the fireplace and prayed he'd leave quickly.

Jack felt as if he'd just kicked a puppy. He picked up his bag, looked at her back. "Goodbye," he said, then walked out the door.

Rachel heard the lock click and hugged herself tightly as the pain poured through her. She would get through this. She had to. She had Alyssa who was depending on her.

Shakily, she began stacking wood in the fireplace. She'd build a fire, make some lunch and— The thought of food set her stomach to churning.

Straightening, she rushed to the bathroom, barely making it in time. She was so sick she didn't have the strength to move, winding up sitting on the floor.

Tomorrow will be better, she told herself. One day at a time.

Rachel struggled with Alyssa's car seat, taking it out of the base belted into the rental car. With the straps of the diaper bag and her purse over one shoulder, she hoisted the portable seat by its handle and hurried inside the sheriff's office. Out of the cold, she turned back the blanket corners, revealing the sleeping baby.

"You're getting heavy," Rachel said softly. "My big girl."

"Can I help you with that, ma'am?" asked a deep, masculine voice.

Rachel looked up at a tall man with dark hair and dark eyes, his smile white in a tanned face with strong features. A fleece-lined denim jacket hung open over wide shoulders, worn jeans, and his boots that looked as if they'd seen a lot of work. In his big, rough hands he held a cowboy hat.

"Have we met?" Rachel asked, thinking she'd remember such a handsome man.

"No, ma'am. I'm Cade Redstone—at your service." He reached for the handle of the car seat, taking it from her easily. "Where are you heading?"

"She's coming to see me," Sloan said from the doorway of the station. Stepping outside, he introduced Rachel to Cade.

Cade smiled at her. "Are you from around here?"

That was a good question, Rachel thought. "For now," she answered.

"Well, in that case, I'd better be inviting my brother up here for a visit right quick," Cade said with a wink. He looked over at Sloan. "Don't want Ryder to miss out on the best-looking women."

"You know Ryder's too busy with his rodeos to come visit the likes of you," Sloan replied through a grin. "Go on, now. Leanne's probably calling you." Taking the baby seat from Rachel, he motioned her into his office. "See ya, buddy," he called to the tall cowboy.

Cade put on his hat, saluted with two fingers to both of them, and went on down the street.

Settling into a chair across from Sloan's desk, Rachel checked Alyssa's covers, making sure she wouldn't be too warm, then looked up at the deputy. "What was it you wanted to see me about?"

"I just wanted to know how you and Alyssa are doing. I would've dropped by your place, but we've been real busy here. Besides, I thought you'd enjoy getting out a little." Sloan knew Jack had left and thought he knew why. Some men weren't the settling-down type. He'd also heard through the small-town grapevine that Rachel had holed up in her little cabin and hadn't stepped out in town in the two weeks since Jack's departure.

"We're doing fine, Sloan," she answered, sounding perhaps a bit too defensive even to her own ears.

"That's good to hear."

Something had occurred to Rachel outside the station. "That man I just met out there, Cade Redstone. He looks as if he has some Native American blood. Have you checked him out as possibly being Alyssa's father?"

Sloan shook his head. "He's not our man. Cade's happily married to Leanne Harding—just got married in September. Besides, he wasn't even around these parts till last May. He's one of Garrett Kincaid's grandsons." He looked at her inquisitively. "Do you know that story?"

"Of Garrett searching for his son Larry's illegitimate children?" Rachel nodded. "Sure, I know. Who in Whitehorn doesn't? But what about his brother?"

Rachel knew she was fishing, but she so desperately needed a lead.

"Ryder? No, he's out on the rodeo circuit. Nothing can hold that man down." He laughed. "Except maybe a two-ton bull."

"I see." Rachel couldn't help but feel disappointed. "So then, I take it you're no further along in the search for Alyssa's father than before?"

"I'm afraid not."

"It's so frustrating! I'd like to keep Alyssa, which would involve some change of plans regarding my job in Chicago, that sort of thing. But if I do all that, decide to remain in Whitehorn and perhaps do freelance work or whatever, I have no assurance that her father won't suddenly reappear and swoop her away."

"You're right." Sloan's face was sympathetic. "I wish I could tell you something more positive. If you want to go back to Chicago, I could look around and maybe find someone to take care of the baby."

"No, no, I don't want that. I—I can manage caring for her alone. It's just that…as you might imagine, each day I love her more. If he comes back—whoever he is—I'm going to find it very hard to give her up." Especially after losing Jack.

"I know. Whoever he is, he's put you in an awkward position. I wish I had a suggestion for you, but we've scoured the Native America community, asked at the res and off. We can't come up with any Native American who was even seen with Christina. And no one's come forth—yet. I think one day someone will, but when…that'll be is anyone's guess. We're no closer to finding her killer, either." He leaned forward, his expression distressed. "I'm frustrated, too."

Rachel understood. "I'm not blaming you, Sloan, or the department. I just feel like I'm in limbo, like I've lost control of my life, my future. I know that sounds dramatic…"

"Not to me it doesn't. My best advice would be don't stay because of the baby. If you really want to live in Whitehorn again, make sure you're staying for the right reasons. Then, should you get permanent custody, she'd be icing on the cake. You know? If there's any way I can help you, Rachel, please let me know."

She gave him a smile. "Thanks, Sloan." She covered the baby with the blanket again, gathered her purse and the diaper bag, and left.

Once outside in the cold air, she let out a trembling sigh. She felt so tired lately, probably a mild depression over her circumstances. But she wasn't giving in to it. Squaring her shoulders, she ignored the car and set off down the street. "We're going to lunch," she told the sleeping child. "It's time we stopped hiding."

It was three in the afternoon and there was a lull at the Hip Hop Café. The lunch crowd was fed and gone, and the dinner folks hadn't yet begun to straggle in. Rachel greeted Janie Austin at the cash register and she made her way to a booth in the back and set the baby carrier down on one side. Removing the blanket, she saw that Alyssa was still asleep. Probably getting out in the fresh air was good for her, as well.

Pulling off her gloves, she sat opposite the baby, plunked down the heavy diaper bag, packed for every emergency, and her purse and shrugged out of her jacket before heaving another weary sigh. She was probably tired from hauling around the baby and the tons of paraphernalia that came along with her wherever she went.

Glancing up, she saw Cade Redstone in a booth on the other side of the café, laughing along with two women. She surmised that the one he sat next to, a real beauty with rich chestnut hair, was his wife. As they sat holding hands, Rachel envied them their good mood and their energy, not to mention their love. I guess marriage does suit some people, she thought.

Listlessly, she picked up the menu. She wasn't really hungry, but she knew she had to eat.

"We haven't seen you here in a while," Janie said, coming over to her booth, order pad in hand.

"It's been so cold, I haven't felt much like going out," Rachel explained. It wasn't exactly the truth, but it would have to do. She had no intention of telling Janie the whole sad story of Jack's leaving her. Then she remembered this was Whitehorn; Janie probably knew all about their breakup, as did everyone in town. News traveled fast in small towns, especially news of a broken heart. "Besides," she continued, "I didn't want Alyssa to catch cold."

Janie peeked into the baby seat, smiling as she

looked over the sleeping child. "She's a real cutie, Rachel. I can see you're taking good care of her."

"Thanks. I try." Rachel liked Janie, who was about her age and married to another deputy, Reed Austin. She managed the Hip Hop with an iron fist in a velvet glove, firm but always kind.

Janie shifted her attention to Rachel. "You're looking a little peaked, though. Can I bring you some coffee or tea while you check out the menu?"

Her morning coffee hadn't set well but maybe some tea would settle her nervous stomach. "Tea would be great," she said. As Janie left, the loving couple across the café found something irresistibly funny. She looked over at them and saw Cade wave. He said something to the women he was with and they all walked over to Rachel's table.

"Afternoon, Rachel. We meet again." Cade put an arm around the pretty brunette and said, "This is my wife, Leanne, and her sister, Daisy Harding."

The new bride extended her hand and shook Rachel's. "Cade tells me he just met you over at the sheriff's office. Would you like to join us?"

Rachel smiled at their kind offer, but declined. "I wouldn't want to ruin your lunch if the baby wakes up." She nodded toward the car seat and the sleeping infant.

Leanne peered over. "She's so beautiful. And I admire you for taking care of her. I didn't know Christina, but I'm sure she's resting peacefully now, knowing you're looking after her daughter." The genuine emotion in Leanne's voice touched Rachel.

"Thank you. I hope so." Tears welled in Rachel's eyes, threatening to spill over. She was so emotional these days.

Leanne touched her hand. "Listen, if you ever want to talk, call me. I have a sister, too, and I can only imagine what you're going through. Let me know if I can do something for you. Anything."

Rachel looked at Daisy. Her hair was pulled back in a twist, which, she suspected, made the quiet woman look older than her years. "Are you from Whitehorn?" she asked.

Daisy shook her head. "No, I'm just visiting my sister for the holidays."

Leanne reached out an arm and hugged her sister. "Cade and I are delighted she's here. We don't get to see nearly enough of her. You know, when I was younger, Daisy took such good care of me. Now I think the best Christmas present I could get is to see her meet a good man—" she looked up at Cade "—and be as happy as I am."

"You keep working on her," Rachel said with a grin. Don't give up on her, she thought. Like I did my sister.

Cade, Leanne and Daisy, after offering their baby-sitting services, said their goodbyes and returned to their table, just as Janie came by to take Rachel's order.

"What's the soup of the day?" Soup was about all Rachel felt her stomach could handle.

"Chicken noodle."

"I'll have a bowl, please, Janie."

"Coming right up." She strolled off, her blond ponytail swinging, just as the door opened and Ellis Montgomery walked in.

Carefully removing his Stetson, Ellis smoothed back his ebony hair as he glanced around the café. When he spotted his daughter at a back booth, his eyes stopped. He stared for several moments, then came to a decision and walked over. "Hello, Rachel," he said, coming up to the booth.

"Hi, dad," she answered quietly.

Almost unwillingly, his eyes swung to the baby, but his expression remained unchanged. "How've you been?"

"Fine. And you?" Talking without saying anything. To think they were reduced to this. Rachel wanted to scream.

"Fine, fine. Max is fine, too. He says he never hears from you."

"Is that right? Well, the gossipmongers being what they are in Whitehorn, I imagine he knows where to find me, and so do you. I wouldn't turn either of you away." She hadn't been able to resist the dig, after all, he'd basically turned her and an innocent child away.

Ellis shifted the Stetson in his hand, clearly uncomfortable. "I heard your investigator fellow went back home without finding out a thing the sheriff's department didn't already know."

"You heard right. The case is still pending."

"So then, he's not coming back?" Ellis asked.

Janie arrived with a tray, preventing Rachel from

answering. Placing the soup and tea fixings on the table in front of Rachel, she smiled. "Anything else I can get you, honey?"

"No, thanks, Janie. This smells good." In reality, the smell was making her stomach queasy, or was it the tension that Ellis's unexpected arrival had created that was chasing away her tenuous appetite? She decided to ignore her father's last question since she really didn't have an answer and picked up her soup spoon, praying her stomach wouldn't rebel.

While Janie had served Rachel's lunch, Ellis again had stared at Alyssa. "Not a thing about Christina do I see in that child," he stated emphatically.

"If you could see her eyes open, you'd agree that they're just like Christina's. But aside from that, the DNA test results are back, as I'm sure the sheriff has told you. Irrefutably, that's your granddaughter." Rachel swallowed soup, her eyes downcast. She'd worded her statement deliberately, knowing he'd hate to hear it put that way. Too bad. He'd have to get used to the idea.

Ellis's face reddened. "You were never difficult like Christina. You were always the good daughter. Why did you change?"

Carefully, Rachel set down her spoon and raised her eyes to her father's face. "Change is necessary. Without change, we don't grow and if we can't grow, we stagnate. The truth is, I didn't change, rather your perception of me did. I have something—no someone worth fighting for here. Someone who can't fight for herself. You ought to try changing, too, Dad. It only hurts for a little while.''

His red face deepened to a dark burgundy, whether with outrage or embarrassment Rachel couldn't have said. Without another word, Ellis stomped to the door and left the café.

She may have gotten the last word, Rachel thought, but she took no pleasure in shaming her father. Perhaps he'd never give up his prejudices, but she could no longer abide his intolerances. If he didn't want anything to do with her because of Alyssa, she'd learn to live with his decision. Sooner or later, a person had to stand up for what she believed.

But Lord, it was wearying. And it left her feeling very alone. Cade and Leanne let out another peal of laughter and Rachel felt a rush of envy. To be carefree, to be married to someone you loved, to have a happy future stretching out before you. How glorious that would be.

However, she'd learned over the past two weeks since Jack had left that it's possible to operate on a surface level with a broken heart. She had a strong will and she wasn't about to let his departure defeat her. The last thing she wanted was that innocent baby girl to pick up on her unhappiness.

Rachel managed to finish nearly the whole bowl of soup and drink half her tea before she bundled up Alyssa, paid her check and climbed back into her rental car. Tomorrow she would call Pete Ambrose and talk with him about her future at Kaleidoscope, she decided.

She had some tough decisions to make. If she remained in Whitehorn because of Alyssa, despite not knowing how long she'd be able to keep her, she couldn't go on not earning an income, not having a job. She'd finished nearly a dozen sketches in and around her cabin and had come up with what she felt was a good story that she'd outlined for a children's book to go with her drawings. Some time ago, she'd met an editor at a publishing house, Donna Hines, who was always looking for the next Dr. Seuss. While Rachel had no illusions that she was that good, she honestly felt she had a chance at publication.

If she was to remain, she'd contact that woman. She also didn't want to keep renting a cabin, she'd prefer buying a house for herself and Alyssa. And buying a car rather than renting one.

So many decisions, Rachel thought as she headed for home. And she felt so tired. Maybe, if Alyssa slept on for a while yet, she could lie down and catch a nap. Then, after a rest, she'd figure out exactly what she should do with the rest of her life.

Ten

Rachel heard someone knocking at her front door and wondered who on earth would be out and about at nine in the morning on a cold and wintry day. For a moment, she thought she might just not answer, hoping whoever it was would go away. She'd been up several times during the night with Alyssa, who was apparently teething, and she hadn't even showered yet. To top things off, she'd just finished a soft boiled egg and toast that threatened to make a reappearance. She had to make a doctor's appointment soon, she decided, shuffling to the door in her slippers, tying the belt of her robe more tightly around her slender frame.

She finally pulled open the door and saw Gina standing on the porch, her red hair windblown, her arms full of packages.

"I wondered where you'd be at this hour," Gina said, smiling as her green eyes swept over Rachel, taking in the disheveled hair, the pale face. "Honey, are you sick?"

"No, no," Rachel answered, standing aside while Gina hurried in out of the cold, dumping her bundles on the couch. "I'm getting a late start this morning.

Alyssa's teething and she kept me up half the night.''
She gestured toward the packages. ''What's all this?''

''Oh, I went shopping for our baby yesterday and
picked up a few things for Alyssa.''

''That's really nice of you. Yes, she's sleeping finally, and I hope she stays that way for a while. Come
into the kitchen and I'll put on water for tea. Or would
you rather have coffee?''

''Tea's fine,'' Gina said, slipping out of the bulky
winter coat that didn't quite fit around her middle
these days. Following Rachel into the kitchen, she sat
at the table while Rachel fussed with the tea fixings.
''I've been meaning to come over, but I had a cold
and I didn't want to give it to Alyssa. How is she?''

''Doing just great, according to the doctor. Growing like a weed. Up until a few days ago when this
tooth started giving her trouble, she rarely cried or
fussed.''

''Poor little thing must be in pain.'' Gina shifted
her weight, trying to sit more comfortably. ''I can tell
you, I'll be glad when this one makes an appearance.
I feel like a grumpy cow these days.''

Rachel shoved back her hair with both hands, wishing she'd have done more than merely run a brush
through it as she sat opposite her friend. ''You look
wonderful,'' she told Gina, meaning it. ''You must
be one of the eighty percent of pregnant women who
glow when they're expecting.''

''Thank you for being kind, but I've gained twenty-
seven pounds and I feel it.'' She studied Rachel's
face, wondering if there was more amiss here than a

little disturbed sleep. Whenever she'd seen Rachel in the past, she'd always been beautifully dressed, her complexion enviable, her hair shining. Now she looked like something the cat dragged home. "Honey, I'm going to be blunt here. You don't look very well. Does this malaise have anything to do with my brother, the jerk?"

Gina had talked with Jack only once since he'd left so abruptly without informing her. Their conversation had been brief and unsatisfactory. Short, curt replies weren't Jack's usual style yet when she'd asked him if anything was wrong, he'd nearly taken off her head, another out-of-character reaction. Which was just one of the reasons that had prompted this visit.

"I don't know what you mean," Rachel answered, averting her eyes and getting up to pour boiling water into a red teapot. "Jack left because the case was at a standstill and he had work back in L.A. waiting for him. He'd met with Sloan often and, although Christina's murder is unsolved and the case is still open, there was nothing more Jack could do here." She'd rehearsed this answer knowing she'd be asked.

Carefully, she carried two cups over, set down the pot, the sugar bowl and a small dish of sliced lemons before resuming her seat. But she still didn't meet Gina's sharp-eyed gaze.

Gina wasn't buying it. "Tell me what really happened, Rachel." She placed her hand over her friend's and squeezed. "I'm not just being nosy. I love my brother, but I know he can be a real jerk."

Rachel felt the tears well up and wiped them away,

shaking her head, unable to say more for fear she'd surely start to cry.

Gina sighed. "You fell in love with him, didn't you? And, let me guess, he warned you not to because he'd one day walk away like our dad did. Am I close?"

Rummaging in the pocket of her robe, Rachel found a tissue and dabbed at her eyes. "Pretty close. Has he done this before?"

"Probably, but I haven't met most of the women he dated. To tell you the truth, he never dates anyone more than once or twice. When he moved in here with you, I was shocked. He's never done that before."

That was small comfort to Rachel right now. "It's my fault, mostly. He warned me, like you said. I even told him that I'd more or less been dumped at the altar myself and wasn't looking for a serious relationship. But...I fell for him anyhow. I don't think it's possible to control these things, although I used to think you could."

"I'm living proof that you can fall in love in an evening, an instant, so don't go beating yourself up over that."

Rachel sniffled into her tissue. "All along, I expected him to leave and, finally, he did." She poured the now steeped tea, added sugar and lemon to hers.

"Our father did walk out and leave us," Gina said. "It was really hard on Mom, but it was harder still on Jack because he was only twelve and suddenly he was the man of the house. Mom is one of those helpless females who can't seem to cope without a man in her life to give her direction and purpose. She more or less sat around for six years and let Jack work two and sometimes three part-time jobs plus go to school. I was only four when Dad left, too young to help much. Jack was breadwinner for us all and father to me. He was wonderful. But it took a toll on him. He's been wary of having to live like that again, I guess.''

Rachel gripped the cup in both hands so tightly her fingers turned white. ''I've heard that story, Gina, and as far as I'm concerned, your father walking out on his family does not mean that one day Jack will do the same. It's not an inherited gene, like a tendency toward brown eyes. So what, now he walks away *before* there's a full family unit, so he won't feel the urge to go later? That's bull.''

Rachel ran out of steam and took several sips of tea. ''He's like a lot of men, afraid of commitment. I just happen to have been unlucky enough to get involved with two like that.''

''Now that I think about it, you're probably right. Jack's always guarded his freedom and acted as if getting married would be the end of everything. However, if it's any consolation, I think he loves you, too.''

Rachel frowned. ''Why would you think that?''

''Not by what he said, but by what he *didn't* say when I last talked to him. He's evasive, which he's never been with me. And he's very grumpy and short-tempered. I believe he'll wake up and realize what he's lost and—''

Gina stopped in midsentence when Rachel suddenly jumped up from the table and ran to the bath-room, her hand over her mouth. Caught off guard, Gina sat still, pondering.

A full five minutes later Rachel came out, her face chalk-white, her hands trembling. "I'm sorry. The tea didn't set well, I guess. I've got a touchy stomach."

Gina didn't speak, just stared at her friend. Finally she decided she'd risk the question. "Rachel, could you be pregnant?"

Rachel burst into tears, her hands going up to cover her face, her slender shoulders shaking as she cried.

Gina moved her chair closer, slipping her arm around Rachel, pulling her close. "Shh, it's all right. We can work this out." Her busy mind whirling this way and that, Gina let her cry it out.

Finally, Rachel stopped, rose to get a box of tissues from the counter, and blew her nose. "I'm sorry," she said. "You must think I'm terrible, pregnant by a man I've only known a few weeks."

"Don't be silly. I told you the story of Trent and me, so who am I to judge? How long have you known?"

"I guess I'm really stupid. I've been throwing up and queasy for weeks, but I thought it was just nerves. Only yesterday did I sit down and figure it out."

"You haven't been to the doctor?"

"No, but I planned on going soon."

"Of course, Jack doesn't know."

Rachel's head came up. "No, and don't you tell him. I mean it."

"I promise I won't. But you should, Rachel."

She shook her head adamantly. "Look, he made it perfectly clear that he had to move on. If he didn't want me alone, then he surely wouldn't want me with a child. You remember you told me you didn't want Trent to know you were expecting because he might think you were trying to blackmail him into a relationship?"

"Yes, I remember. But it's *Jack's* child."

"Yes, I know that. But I can manage quite well raising the baby without him or any man. And I can take care of Alyssa, as well. Honestly, Gina, Jack didn't ask to be a father and he'd probably hate it if he knew. This way, at least he doesn't hate me. I'll handle it on my own. I've got investments. We won't starve. The last thing I want is some man to feel responsible for me or my baby."

Gina sat back, admiring her enormously. "You're really something, you know." Her busy mind was racing toward a probable solution. "Any chance that the guy who left you at the altar may come looking for you?"

"Richard Montrose?" Rachel sent her an incredulous look. "None whatsoever, nor would I want him if he did. Honestly, I don't want you worrying about us. We'll be fine."

Finishing the last of her tea, Gina rose. "I've got to run, but I'll be back." She leaned down to hug Rachel. "Remember, call me if you need anything. We're family."

Rachel gave her the first real smile she'd genuinely felt in ages. "Thanks for that." She walked her to the door, gesturing toward the packages. "And for all those. My goodness, you're quite the little shopper."

"I love buying baby things." Gina struggled back into her coat and opened the door. "Don't be a stranger. Call me after you've been to see the doctor, promise?"

Rachel smiled. "I promise."

After she left, Rachel went in to clean up the kitchen. Finishing, she hoped she'd have time to take a quick shower before Alyssa woke up. But as she walked into her bedroom, she heard the baby crying her hungry cry.

"No rest for the weary," Rachel said out loud as she walked back into the kitchen to heat a bottle.

Jack locked the door to his office in a high-rise office building a couple blocks off Sunset Boulevard, thinking he should be feeling elated. He'd wrapped up a very difficult case he'd been working on for months, begun weeks before his trips to Whitehorn. The client had been most appreciative, handing him a generous check. Ronnie Drake, his partner who'd worked with him less than a year, had also scored big this afternoon, closing out an ongoing case.

Ronnie had asked him to leave early with him and they'd go celebrate. Jack had begged off. Despite the fact that the business was doing very well, thank you, he didn't feel like celebrating.

Where was the pleasure, the satisfaction, in jobs well done, in succeeding? Damned if he knew.

Frowning, he pushed the button for the elevator and

waited impatiently. Why was he so impatient lately? He asked himself. He had nothing to run home to, no one waiting, no dinner that would be ruined if he stayed out half the night. Which is the way he liked it, he reminded himself.

The elevator doors slid silently open and he got on, distracted by his errant thoughts.

"Hello, Jack," a warm feminine voice from behind greeted him.

Turning, he recognized Sharon What's-her-name, a lovely blonde he'd dated occasionally last year. He gave her a smile while he tried to remember her last name. "Hi. How's it going?"

"Not bad. How are things with you?" She was lovely, model-thin, her hair pulled back in some sleek hairdo that showed off her wonderful cheekbones. She wore gorgeous clothes, today's outfit in forest green, expensive-looking. She was exactly like dozens of others he'd dated over the years. Beautiful, stylish, undemanding.

"Fine, fine." Jack cleared his throat, realizing he had absolutely nothing more he wanted to say to Sharon.

The elevator stopped at another floor and more people boarded. Jack and Sharon stepped back.

"I haven't seen you around much," she purred.

"I've been out of town quite a bit on a case." He sent her a quick, apologetic glance, then faced the front.

The elevator doors slid open on the main floor. Always a gentleman, Jack waited until everyone else got off, then stepped out. He saw that she'd lingered and wished she hadn't.

"Have you got plans tonight?" Sharon asked, silky smooth. "We could stop in P.J.'s for a drink. For old times' sake."

"Thanks, but I've got an appointment," he lied. "Rain check?" he asked, hoping to salvage her pride.

"Sure." Cool and seemingly unaffected, she smiled. "See you later." Leaving a trail of expensive cologne, she left through the double glass doors.

Jack heaved a sigh of relief as he walked over and bought a newspaper from the newsstand in the lobby. Leaving the building, he walked two blocks to the lot where his BMW was parked, got in and headed for his west side condo, too lost in thought to be annoyed at the usual rush-hour congestion. Or to notice the warmth of the winter day, the weather still in the seventies.

Twenty minutes later, he eased his car into the underground parking garage, got out and took the elevator up to the twelfth floor. Digging in his pocket, he found his keys, then stood staring at the gold-and-onyx keychain Rachel had given him. Why was it so many things reminded him of her, each time throwing him off balance?

Stopping in front of No. 1214, he was about to enter when a woman got off the elevator carrying a baby. Normally, Jack would have barely spared a glance toward a mother and child, but something made him smile and say hello as she approached.

She stopped, friendly-like. "Hello." She was attractive, somewhere in her mid-twenties with light brown hair and freckles on her nose.

Jack's gaze went to the baby in the pink blanket, a round-faced little girl without a hair on her head. "How old is she?" he asked, surprising himself.

"Five months yesterday," the woman told him proudly. "She's already got a tooth." With a finger, she parted the baby's little lips and showed off the new acquisition.

She was cute, but not nearly as pretty as Alyssa, Jack thought. Nor was the mother anywhere close to being as attractive as Rachel. Knowing she was waiting for a comment, he obliged. "A tooth already? I didn't know babies had teeth at five months." Alyssa was the same age. Was she teething already?

"Some do, some don't." The woman shifted her heavy bundle and, with a smile, said goodbye and walked down the hallway past Jack's place.

Inserting his key at last, he went inside and flipped on a light. His housekeeper had been in today and the place smelled of lemon polish, not unpleasant. Taking off his jacket and tie as he walked to the kitchen, he opened the refrigerator and took out the orange juice. He poured himself a tall glass, drinking it as he looked around. A designer kitchen, it had all the amenities he'd felt he needed, yet seldom used. He could cook, had had to learn at an early age. But mostly, he ate out or brought in takeout.

He opened the refrigerator again, feeling slightly hungry, wondering what to fix, but seeing nothing that appealed to him. As if in flashback, he remembered the great meals Rachel used to make. Pot roast, a chicken-and-rice dish, shrimp and pasta. He'd eaten like a king in that little nine-by-twelve kitchen. He shut the refrigerator door, his appetite leaving him.

He walked back into his living room. ''Oatmeal'' the decorator had called the color of the carpeting throughout his condo. The walls were champagne. Colors it would seem were all connected to food or drink these days. His oversize mocha-brown leather couch faced a ceiling-to-floor bank of windows that looked out on the lights of L.A. In the corner was a fireplace he'd never used. Looking around, he saw that every toss pillow was placed just so, every book on the shelves was neatly in place, spine facing out. The lighting was subdued and, with the flick of a button, he could activate his stereo and music would fill each room.

Walking to his bedroom, he stared at his king-size bed that he'd been tossing and turning in all alone for the past couple of weeks. Here again was a perfect room designed for the professional that he was, the president of his own company, earning well into six figures at age thirty-five. He entered his walk-in closet where suits and shirts hung on one side, casual attire on the other. Below were his shoes, from formal to sportswear, all polished, ready for any activity he chose. Above were some hats, a Stetson that Gina had given him for standing up in her wedding, baseball hats, fun hats for a fun guy.

A fun guy was something he hadn't been in a long while. Jack drained his juice, set the glass on his nightstand and lay back on his bed, kicking off his tassel loafers. He was living the American dream, successful, monied, with all the grown-up toys his income could buy. He'd worked hard, paid his dues and was now prepared to reap the rewards.

Only his list of rewards had grown stale and so had he.

Raising his arms, he placed both hands under his head and stared at the ceiling. *Do you know what you want?* Rachel had asked him. And Jack had thought he did. He wanted what he had, with no demands on his time he wasn't willing to give, no commitments to others, no ties except to his sister and, occasionally, his mother. He had the perfect life, the good life.

So then, what in hell was he unhappy about?

Closing his eyes, he saw himself painting Alyssa's bedroom, putting together her crib, laughing with Rachel when he'd put the wheels on backward. They'd laughed a lot—when shopping for groceries, cleaning up after dinner together, or sitting in front of the fire eating pizza off paper plates. He remembered Alyssa's wide eyes when they'd driven around to look at the Christmas lights. But most of all, he relived in his mind the magical hours he'd spent in the four-poster with Rachel.

Rachel. His heart skipped several beats at the very thought of her. What had she done to him? She'd ruined his perfect life. If she wasn't in it, it was no longer perfect. Plain and simple. But how could he protect her from himself? Wasn't it kinder to leave her now rather than later when the wanderlust he'd inherited from his father took over?

Or was he using that as an excuse, as Rachel had said, because he truly was afraid of marriage and all that entailed? *Why can't you be honest, at least?* she'd asked. *Quit blaming your father for everything.* He had been doing that, hadn't he?

Disgusted with himself, with this line of thinking, Jack sat up, found the remote and clicked on the big-screen TV opposite the bed. It took him a few moments to realize they were playing a documentary on Montana. Annoyed, he turned the set off.

He needed to think things through. But first, a jog on the beach to clear his mind. He was stripped down to his briefs when the phone rang. He grabbed the bedroom extension. "Hello?"

"Jack, it's Gina."

Her voice sounded odd. "Gina, are you all right? Is the baby…?"

"We're both fine. I haven't talked to you in a while, so I'm just calling to see how *you* are."

"I'm fine. Busy. Wrapped up a big case today. I was just going out to jog on the beach. It's seventy here. I'll bet you're freezing your fanny over there."

Well, at least he wasn't giving her monosyllabic answers. "Yeah, it's pretty cold." She saw no reason to beat around the bush. "Have you talked with Rachel lately?"

Jack sat on the bed. He'd been avoiding calls from his sister for this very reason. "No, should I have?"

"Yeah, I think you should. I was over to see her and Alyssa yesterday and—"

"How are they?" The question had slipped out.

Aha! Gotcha! Gina smiled. "Alyssa's teething. Rachel looks wonderful. She's expecting a guest." It wasn't exactly a lie.

"Oh? Who might that be?"

Gina shot a glance heavenward, hoping she'd be forgiven a white lie for a good cause. "You remember hearing about Richard Montrose, the man she was engaged to? Well, he's back from Italy and a big success with his paintings. He called her, asking her to forgive him, and said he's planning on visiting her in Whitehorn." Fingers crossed, she waited for her brother's response.

Jack was silent, thinking that over. "You don't say. I got the impression she didn't have any feelings left for him."

"Oh, she says she doesn't, but she's letting him come anyhow." Gina waited, but he was quiet, probably thinking hard. "You know, you could change all that, Jack."

"What do you mean?"

"Oh, come now. Let's remember who you're talking with here. I may be your younger sister, but I can read you like a book. You care about Rachel very deeply. I know you went home to think about things. Well, Jack, do you think you have unlimited chances, unlimited time to figure things out?"

Still no reply, so she went on. "Look at your life there, Jack. You go to bed alone, wake up alone, eat alone. Sure, you have friends and probably lots of dates, if you want them. But do any of those women mean anything to you? Is this how you pictured your ideal life? I know, you're a big successful businessman. But money ain't everything, sweetie. It's damn hard to snuggle up to cold, hard cash on a winter's night.''

"All right, I get the picture. Do you really think this guy has a chance with her? I mean, it's been years and—''

"You never know. Rachel's the forgiving sort. Besides, if she winds up with full custody of Alyssa, she may well remain in Whitehorn and she'll need help raising her. How do you feel about that baby?'' This was a loaded question, but one Gina had to know the answer to.

"I'm surprised to say I fell in love with her. She's so happy all the time, so responsive, you know.'' He cleared his throat, realizing what he'd just said. Yet realizing he meant it.

"Jack,'' Gina said, her voice softening, "answer something for me. Were you happy here with Rachel?'' After all, she really didn't want to push him into something he'd regret.

Happy? It wasn't even hard to admit that he'd never been that happy before or since. Then what had he run from? Jack asked himself. Probably the only real and lasting happiness he'd ever known, came the answer. "Yeah, I was.''

"I know you're afraid you'll turn out as irresponsible as Dad was. But look at the facts, Jack. You've never done an irresponsible thing in your life. You took care of Mom and me, you gave up your youth and fun years for us. You took me into the company and always looked after me. What makes you think you'll change suddenly into this irresponsible jerk?''

''Okay, okay. When you're right, you're right.''

Gina couldn't help smiling. ''Does that mean you're coming here to see Rachel?''

''When is Richard arriving?'' Suddenly it occurred to Jack that he might be too late.

''Not for a while. You've got time, but not a lot. Don't drive. Catch a plane and I'll meet you.''

''No, I'll rent a car like before. I'll call for reservations right now.''

''Good. You won't regret this, Jack.''

''I know, and thanks. I love you. See you soon.''

''I love you, too.'' Gina hung up the phone and let out a whoop of delight. Then she went to search out Trent to tell him what she'd done.

Rachel carried Alyssa to her bed and put her down for her afternoon nap. Fortunately, the tooth had broken through and the baby was once more her smiling self. Sighing, she walked back into the living room and lit the fire she'd laid before leaving for her doctor's appointment. Even though she was wearing a white turtleneck and her gray wool slacks, she was chilled. Small wonder since it was well below freezing outside. The Montana winter was in full swing with about six inches of fresh snow on the ground from yesterday's storm.

Kicking off the slippers she'd put on after removing her boots, she reached for the afghan on the back of the couch and snuggled down under it. Alyssa would sleep for a good two hours, giving Rachel time to rest, as well. The doctor had told her to take it easy and he'd given her a huge bottle of prenatal vitamins. Otherwise, he'd said, she was a very healthy woman and there was no reason to believe she wouldn't deliver a healthy baby.

Pregnant. It was stunning news, even though she'd been fairly certain she was. A tiny boy or girl. Who would the baby look like? A boy who looked like Jack might be difficult to handle, a constant reminder of the man who'd walked away. Yet at least she'd have a little something of him with her.

Yesterday she'd called Kaleidoscope and talked with Pete Ambrose. He'd sounded genuinely sorry she was quitting, but he said he understood, though he really didn't, certain she was nuts for moving to a small town in Montana after years in the big city. However, Rachel knew she was staying for all the right reasons. Not for Alyssa, though the baby would have a home with her for as long as she needed one. Not for Jack, either. For herself.

Perhaps there really was no place like home. And you *could* go home again, if you were ready. Rachel thought she was ready. No more rat race in the world of graphic design. She'd also called Donna Hines, the children's book editor she'd met, and been enormously pleased that the woman remembered her. She said she'd love to see her new project.

It was a start and it was something she'd always wanted to do. The type of work she could do anywhere, really. But being back in Montana felt right. Maybe, in time, Dad would come around. She needed to make more of an effort with Max, hopefully to rekindle what they'd once had. Then there was Gina, who was turning out to be a marvelous friend. They had a lot in common. And perhaps she'd look up some of her other friends from the past, Rachel thought.

In the spring, she'd look for a house to buy. Meanwhile, she had Alyssa and her work. She still missed Jack, but she was trying to accept his departure. She would learn in time to be happy without him.

Stretching out, she just got comfortable and closed her eyes when she heard a knock at the door. Thinking it was probably Gina who knew she'd had a doctor's appointment today, Rachel got up and went to open the door.

He stood there in a sheepskin jacket, wearing a hesitant smile, blue jeans and boots, and on his head a black Stetson. Her heart skidded and skipped before settling to a fast beat. He looked so damned good, she was speechless.

Jack took off his hat, held it in hands none too steady. "It's pretty cold out here. Do you think I could come in?" She was every bit as beautiful as he'd been remembering in his restless dreams. Her dark hair just brushed the shoulders of her sweater, her blue eyes were suspicious and her mouth was unsmiling. He'd change all that, he vowed.

Rachel stepped back to let him in, then closed the door, leaning against it for support. Why had he come back? That was the big question. "Did you miss the snow? Is that why you're back?"

"It wasn't the snow I missed." He stomped the white stuff off his boots before removing his jacket. Stepping close to her, he met her unwavering stare. "It's you. I missed you."

She pressed her back into the door, knowing if he touched her she'd be lost. "For how long this time, Jack?"

She wasn't going to make it easy for him. "Forever, if you'll have me." He took her hand, found it stiff and unyielding. "The thing is, I have this great life in L.A., work I enjoy, a racy little sportscar, a terrific office, a beautifully decorated condo, everything I'd ever thought I wanted." He leaned closer, still not touching anywhere but her hand. "Then I met you and it all became meaningless. I realized none of it's any good without you. Those things, they're the icing on the cake. But you, Rachel, you're the cake." He watched her eyes, saw that she was still wary, but softening a little.

"And this came to you suddenly one morning?"

"No. It came to me after weeks of suddenly realizing my life there is shallow, that I can't enjoy it because there's something missing. You." He dared to place his hands on her waist. "You make it all come together for me, if that doesn't sound too corny. All I did was sit around thinking, remembering all the good things we had here, the fun, the laughter. The love.'' He'd played the ace card and waited.

Rachel's heart was pounding so hard she was surprised it wasn't leaping out of her chest. Could she be hearing correctly? These kinds of things only happened in the movies or books. ''Love,'' she said slowly, drawing out the word. ''I don't believe you ever mentioned that word in connection with me.''

''I didn't, but I'm mentioning it now. I love you, Rachel. I want to marry you, to spend the rest of my life with you. I've grown to love Alyssa, too. I want to take care of both of you.''

''Don't!'' she said on a near sob. ''Please don't lead me on or lie to me, not about this. I—I've never loved like this before. I can't handle it if you're just saying what you think I want to hear.''

More sure of himself after hearing her, he took her hands. ''I'm saying exactly what I believe. You once told me that what the mind can conceive and believe, it can achieve. Love may have started in my mind, but it's moved into my heart now, and it's here to stay.'' He pulled her into his arms and buried his face in her sweet-smelling hair. ''I can't bear the thought of you going back to Chicago with Richard.''

Richard? Where had that come from? Never mind, she'd ask him later, Rachel decided. But one thing couldn't wait.

She pulled back from him and gazed into his eyes. ''There's something I have to tell you, Jack.''

''Anything, as long as you say you love me back.''

How was she going to find the words? She'd often fantasized that he'd come back to her and she'd find a way to tell him about her pregnancy, but she'd never really let herself indulge in the mind game. It hurt too much. "I—" She stopped, then blurted it out. "I'm pregnant."

She averted her gaze, not daring to look at him, not wanting to see his reaction if it wasn't the one she'd hoped for. But she knew she had to face it. She looked at him and saw the smile start at his lips and eventually rise to his eyes. "I'm going to be a father..." he said, as if feeling out the words.

"How do you feel about that?" she asked. She'd seen him with Alyssa that night in the rocker, and she knew how good he was with her, how he'd held her, crooned to her. She also knew how protective he felt toward Gina's expected baby. She hoped...

"I feel...good," he said. He cupped her face in his palms and lowered his mouth to hers in a gentle kiss of so much promise that Rachel felt tears well in her eyes.

"Say you'll take me back, Rachel," he whispered when he finally broke the kiss. "There's no place I want to be but here with you." He dropped a feather-light kiss onto her lips. "And Alyssa." He kissed her cheek. "And our baby. I want to make a home with you. A family."

There was so much they had yet to discuss, such as her decision to stay in Whitehorn, some problems to work on, some compromises to make. But for now she only knew that she was exactly where she wanted to be, back in Jack's arms.

She smiled at him through the tears that trickled down her cheeks. "Welcome home, Jack."

MONTANA BRIDES
continues with

ONE WEDDING NIGHT
by Karen Hughes,
also on the shelves this month.

Turn the page for an exciting preview…

One Wedding Night

by

Karen Hughes

The country music blaring from the jukebox inside the Hitching Post, a popular watering hole on the outskirts of San Antonio, didn't make conversation easy. But Ryder Redstone wasn't interested in conversation. He hadn't been interested in much of anything since the night of his half brother's wedding reception in September. Usually calf roping and the rodeo circuit kept him keyed up, ready to tackle the next competition.

Tomorrow morning he was leaving for California to compete for a substantial purse and a brand-new truck. But even that thought didn't get his adrenaline flowing. It seemed like only thoughts of Daisy Harding did. That one night they'd spent together...

Since that night he'd frequently had to shrug off the vision of her face as he'd discovered she was a virgin, as well as the memories of the pleasure that had overtaken them both. A thirty-year-old virgin! At first he'd been astonished, then particularly pleased until he'd awakened to find her gone. Since then, he'd kicked himself up and down. After all, Daisy was his new sister-in-law's sister.

You're spending entirely too much time thinking about a woman you might never see again.

Looking for a distraction, he caught sight of a blonde standing at the end of the bar. He'd spotted her here a couple of times before. She was a looker, with her curly hair, blue eyes and tight jeans.

Suddenly the bartender yelled for Ryder and pointed to the phone.

Immediately worried that something was amiss with his parents at Rimrock Ranch—he'd told them he was stopping here—he scraped back his chair and strode quickly to the phone.

"How much are you going to win in San Diego this time?" It was his half brother Cade.

He and Cade had their mother's Cheyenne blood in common. Ryder's birth father, who'd been a good father to Cade too, was also Cheyenne. The bonds of heritage united the family in a way nothing else could. "I'm going to win a shiny crew cab along with enough money to see me through the year."

"Whew! High stakes. How about doing me a favor afterward?"

Cade was the responsible older brother, steady, now married and settled down. The illegitimate son of a deceased Montana landowner, Cade had been called to Whitehorn by his newfound grandfather last spring to receive his legacy. He'd decided to stay a month or so to get to know Garrett Kincaid and other members of his family, as well as to forget about a fiancée who'd left him at the altar. Instead he'd met Leanne Harding, married her, and was now building a life there. He wouldn't be asking for a favor if he didn't need one.

"Trouble?" Ryder asked. The Kincaid ranch where Cade was living had seen its share.

"Everything's fine, but I'd like you to come up and start some green colts that I bought. Within the next week or so we're going to have our hands full with calving. You could help out with that in your spare time."

Ryder laughed. There was no spare time on a ranch, especially not on one the size of the Kincaid spread.

February and March were slow months for rodeo-ing. He could give Cade some of his time if that's what he needed. "Sure I can get them started. But don't you have someone to help out?" Ryder remembered a tall, brooding, blond wrangler who'd kept his distance from Ryder whenever he'd visited Cade.

"I don't like the way he handles the horses. He could learn a lot from you."

"I'm no teacher," Ryder said. "You know that."

"Yeah, I know. Everything you do, you do by in-stinct. But just watching you around the horses might help Watts get the hang of how I intend to handle training around here."

Ryder planned to leave tomorrow morning to drive to San Diego. Add on five days for the rodeo, another four or five to get back up to Montana. "I'll be there in about two weeks. Is that okay?"

"That's great. And good luck in California. I'll be watching for that new truck."

Ryder grinned as he said goodbye, and his gaze rested again on the woman still standing by the bar. Her blue eyes looked into his brown ones as friendly as all get-out. Why sit alone when he could have the company of a pretty woman? And maybe more.

But as he ambled toward her, he saw Daisy Harding's face once more. If his visit to Cade lasted long enough, he might run into her again.

Or he might not.

He told himself it didn't matter.

* * * *

Don't forget
ONE WEDDING NIGHT
is on the shelves now.

Escape into

Just a few pages
into any Silhouette®
novel and you'll find
yourself escaping
into a world of
desire and intrigue,
sensation and
passion.

Silhouette

Diana Palmer — *Beloved*

Rebecca York — *Nowhere Man*

The Marriage Bargain — Jennifer Mikels

A Husband Waiting To Happen — MARIE FERRARELLA

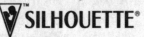

Danger, deception and desire

♥™ SILHOUETTE
INTRIGUE™

Enjoy these dynamic mysteries with a
thrilling combination of breathtaking
romance and heart-stopping suspense.
Unexpected plot twists and
page-turning writing will keep you
on the edge of your seat.

Four new titles every month
available from the
READER SERVICE™
on subscription